THE OXFORD M·E·R·R·Y CHRISTMAS BOOK

Written and designed
by Rita Winstanley

Oxford University Press
Oxford Toronto Melbourne

Contents

Merry Christmas from Oxford

To my husband Roger

Oxford University Press, Walton Street, Oxford OX2 6DP

Oxford
New York   Toronto   Melbourne   Auckland
Petaling Jaya   Singapore   Hong Kong   Tokyo
Delhi   Bombay   Calcutta   Madras   Karachi
Nairobi   Dar es Salaam   Cape Town
and associated companies in
Beirut   Berlin   Ibadan   Nicosia

OXFORD is a trade mark of Oxford University Press

This arrangement and selection Oxford University Press
1987

First published 1987

British Library Cataloguing in Publication Data
Winstanley, Rita
Happy Christmas.
1. Christmas — Juvenile literature
I. Title
394.2'68282   GT4985.5
ISBN 0-19-278120-0

Printed in Hong Kong

Acknowledgements

The author and publisher wish to thank the following for permission to use extracts from copyright material:

Hans Andersen: 'The Fir Tree'. From L W Kingsland: *Hans Andersen's Fairy Tales* (OUP 1985). © L W Kingsland 1985. **Rachel Anderson:** 'The girl shepherd'. © Rachel Anderson 1987. Reprinted by permission of the author. **Rodney Bennett:** 'Robins song'. From *Come Follow Me by Rodney Bennett. Reprinted by permission of Mrs Bennett.* **U A Fanthorpe:** 'What the donkey saw'. First published in *Poems for Christmas* (Harry Chambers/Peterloo Poets, 1981). Reprinted by permission of the author. **Michael Harrison:** 'Baldur'. From Harrison: *The Doom of the Gods* (OUP 1985). © Michael Harrison 1985. **E V Knox:** 'The Spanish Main'. Reprinted by permission of *Punch*. **Wes Magee:** 'Carolling around the estate'. © Wes Magee 1985. Reprinted by permission of the author. **Walter de la Mare:** 'Snowflake'. Reprinted by permission of the Literary Trustees of Walter de la Mare, and the Society of Authors as their representative. **Barbara Leonie Picard:** 'The Stories of Plouhinec'. From Barbara Leonie Picard: *French Legends, Tales and Fairy Stories* (OUP 1955). Reprinted by permission of Oxford University Press. **Charles G D Roberts:** 'Ice'. From *Selected Poems* (1936) by Charles G D Roberts. Reprinted by permission of The Ryerson Press, Toronto. **L Scott:** 'Advent'. From Isobel Armstrong and Roger Mansfield: *A Sudden Line* (OUP 1976). Reprinted by permission of Oxford University Press. **William Kean Seymour:** 'Making the most of it'. From William Kean Seymour: *Happy Christmas* (Burke Publishing Co Ltd, 1968). Reprinted by permission of the author. © William Kean Seymour 1968. **Kit Wright:** 'The budgie's New Year message'. From *Hot Dog and Other Poems* by Kit Wright (Kestrel Books, 1981), page 35, copyright © 1981 by Kit Wright. **Lynn Zirkel:** 'The snowman'. © Lynn Zirkel 1987. Reprinted by permission of the author.

The publishers have made every effort to trace and contact copyright holders, but in some cases without success. Should any infringement have occurred, the publishers tender their apologies and will rectify any omission in future editions of this book.

The publishers wish to thank the following for supplying photographic material and information:

Barnaby's Picture Library: p.68/69, p.85; **BBC Hulton Picture Library:** p.85; **Neil Bromhall:** p.12/13; **Camerapix Hutchison:** p.94; **Christmas Archives:** p.74, p.90/91; **Mary Evans Picture Library:** p.18, p.20, p.25, p.31, p.33, p.36, p.56/57, p.57, p.60/61, p.89; **Susan Griggs/David Beatty:** p.34; **Hong Kong Tourist Association:** p.90/91; **Oxford Scientific Films/Richard Packwood:** p.46; **Promotion Australia, London:** p.102; **David Richardson:** p.93; **Brian Shuel:** p.21, p.64, p.85.

Studio photography by: Chris Honeywell.

With special thanks to Rosemarie Pitts for all her help.

Illustrations by: Judith Allibone, Rowan Barnes-Murphy, John Bendall, Ann Blockley, Pete Bowman, Penny Dann, Bob Dewar, Tina Hancocks, Nick Harris, Sue Heap, Tudor Humphries, Tony Morris, Paddy Mounter, Julie Ormston, David Parkins, Viv Quillin, Nick Sharratt, Helen Stringer, Martin White, Freire Wright.

Cover by: Tudor Humphries

BEFORE YOU START

BEFORE YOU START MAKING ANY OF THE THINGS IN THIS BOOK, I THINK I OUGHT TO WARN YOU. IF YOU DON'T WANT TO GET TO THE END OF THE BOOK LOOKING...

LIKE THIS... **OR THIS...** **OR EVEN THIS...**

THEN YOU HAD BETTER READ THE NEXT TWO PAGES VERY CAREFULLY. YES, I KNOW THAT YOU WOULD RATHER GET ON WITH READING THE REST OF THE BOOK, BUT **DON'T SAY I DIDN'T WARN YOU!**

WHEN YOU ARE COOKING

MELTING CHOCOLATE

WHEN CHOCOLATE MELTS, IT BECOMES SMOOTH AND SHINY. IF IT GETS TOO HOT IT GOES LUMPY AND HARD AND NO AMOUNT OF BEATING WITH A WOODEN SPOON WILL MAKE IT SHINY AGAIN. THIS MEANS THAT YOU WILL HAVE WASTED GOOD CHOCOLATE, SO REMEMBER TO MELT IT IN A BASIN OVER A PAN OF HOT BUT NOT BOILING WATER. IT TAKES LONGER BUT IT'S WORTH IT.

ADDING COLOUR AND FLAVOUR

COLOURINGS AND FLAVOURINGS ARE VERY CONCENTRATED. A FEW DROPS MEANS ONLY 1 OR 2. YOU CAN SPOIL WHAT YOU ARE MAKING BY ADDING TOO MUCH. START BY ADDING A DROP AT A TIME, YOU CAN ALWAYS ADD MORE.

SEPARATING EGG YOLKS

IF YOU DON'T WANT TO BE EATING SCRAMBLED EGGS FOR THE REST OF THE WEEK, THEN I SUGGEST THAT YOU ASK SOMEONE TO SEPARATE EGGS FOR YOU.

IF YOU INSIST ON DOING IT YOURSELF, THEN BREAK THE EGG ONTO A SAUCER AND PUTTING A SMALL GLASS, OR AN EGG CUP OVER THE YOLK, POUR THE EGG WHITE INTO A BASIN.

Julie O.

WHEN YOU ARE MAKING THINGS

TRANSFERRING SHAPES TO CARD.

1ST TRACE THE SHAPE FROM THE BOOK ONTO SOMETHING THAT YOU CAN SEE THROUGH, SUCH AS TRACING PAPER OR GREASEPROOF PAPER. WHEN YOU HAVE DONE THIS, TURN THE TRACING OVER, AND WITH A SOFT PENCIL, SCRIBBLE OVER ALL THE LINES. TURN IT OVER AGAIN, POSITION ON CARD OR PAPER AND DRAW OVER THE LINES AGAIN.

CUTTING WITH A CRAFT KNIFE.

DON'T ASK A GROWN UP TO DO IT FOR YOU. THAT WAY IF ANYONE IS GOING TO CUT THEMSELVES, IT WON'T BE YOU.

SCORING CARD.

IF YOU TRY TO FOLD CARDBOARD IN A STRAIGHT LINE, THE FOLD WILL BE ALL WIGGLY, UNLESS YOU SCORE IT FIRST. ALL THAT SCORING MEANS IS MAKING A DENT IN THE CARD WITHOUT CUTTING IT, SO THAT WHEN YOU FOLD IT, IT KNOWS WHERE TO FOLD. YOU DO THIS BY HOLDING A RULER AGAINST THE EDGE THAT YOU WANT TO FOLD, THEN WITH AN ORDINARY KITCHEN KNIFE (THE SORT THAT YOU USE AT MEALTIMES), DRAW IT DOWN THE EDGE OF THE RULER, PRESSING IT INTO THE CARD. THIS WON'T CUT THE CARD, BUT WHEN YOU FOLD IT, THE CREASE WILL BE STRAIGHT.

SPRAY PAINT.

BE CAREFUL. DON'T SPRAY INSIDE THE HOUSE. NOT ONLY WILL THE SPRAY PAINT GET ALL OVER THE WALLS, CARPET, DOG, HAMSTER... BUT YOU WILL FEEL SICK AND DIZZY IF YOU BREATHE TOO MUCH OF THE STUFF IN.

GLUE

READ THE INSTRUCTIONS ON THE PACKET. SOME GLUE WILL STICK PAPER BUT WOULD BE NO GOOD FOR FELT OR CARDBOARD. SOME "EXTRA STRONG" GLUES CAN BE DANGEROUS, SO DON'T USE THEM, THEY WILL STICK ALMOST ANYTHING, AND THAT INCLUDES YOU! NONE OF THE 'THINGS TO MAKE' IN THIS BOOK NEED GLUE THAT STRONG ANYWAY, SO AVOID THEM.

Julie O.

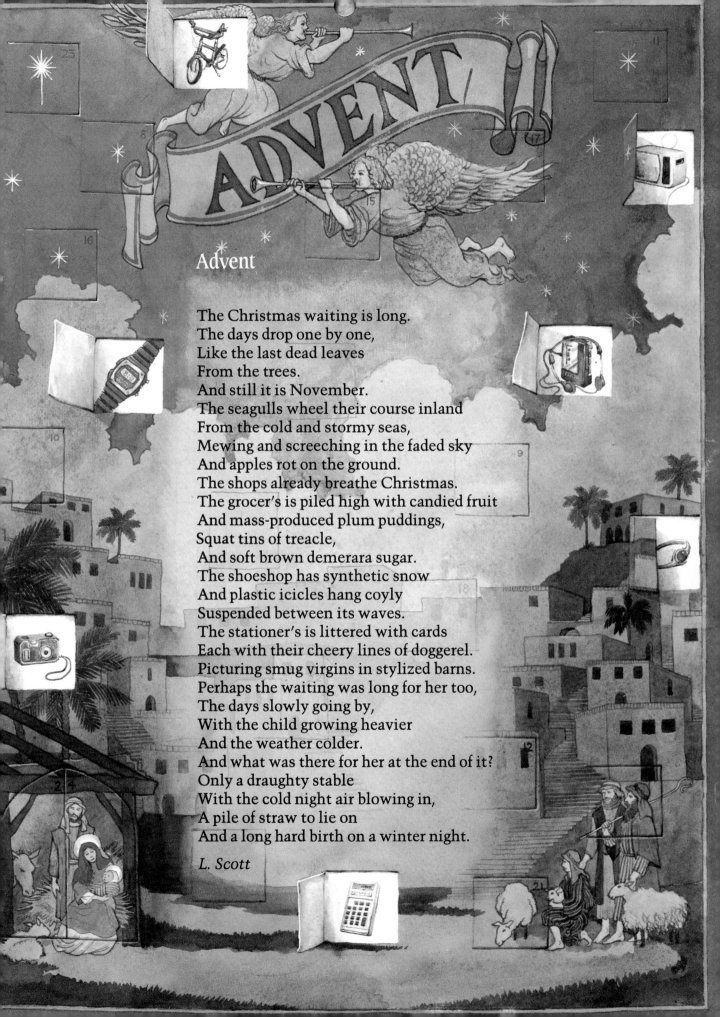

Advent

The Christmas waiting is long.
The days drop one by one,
Like the last dead leaves
From the trees.
And still it is November.
The seagulls wheel their course inland
From the cold and stormy seas,
Mewing and screeching in the faded sky
And apples rot on the ground.
The shops already breathe Christmas.
The grocer's is piled high with candied fruit
And mass-produced plum puddings,
Squat tins of treacle,
And soft brown demerara sugar.
The shoeshop has synthetic snow
And plastic icicles hang coyly
Suspended between its waves.
The stationer's is littered with cards
Each with their cheery lines of doggerel.
Picturing smug virgins in stylized barns.
Perhaps the waiting was long for her too,
The days slowly going by,
With the child growing heavier
And the weather colder.
And what was there for her at the end of it?
Only a draughty stable
With the cold night air blowing in,
A pile of straw to lie on
And a long hard birth on a winter night.

L. Scott

Advent

The weeks before Christmas are full of excitement. People rush about shopping for presents, decorating their houses, sending cards, and generally getting ready for the coming holiday.

Advent (which means 'coming') begins on 1 December. In the Church this is the time when people fast and pray while remembering the long journey that Mary and Joseph had to make to Bethlehem.

Decorations have been used for many years to add to this feeling of anticipation. In many churches candles are lit on the four Sundays before Christmas.

A German custom which we adopted in this country is the making of an Advent crown. This is a wreath of evergreens hung from the ceiling, and decorated with four candles. One of these candles is lit on each of the Sundays up to Christmas, until on the fourth Sunday they are all alight.

Another type of decoration used at this time is the Advent calendar. This also came originally from Germany. The early calendars were pictures with twenty-four windows cut in them. Behind each window there was a small present or sweet. Today our Advent calendars have pictures behind the windows, the last is always the nativity scene which is opened on Christmas Eve.

Before the Puritans banned all Christmas celebrations (in 1644), a model of Mary and Jesus used to be taken from house to house. The occupants would give a small amount of money to bring them good luck in the following year.

In Germany a type of cake is baked during Advent called a Christstollen. When cooked, this cake is covered with white icing to look like the baby Jesus wrapped in swaddling clothes.

an Advent calendar

Why not try making an Advent calendar for one of your friends, or a younger brother or sister?

The one shown here can be filled with surprises (or shocks), and will add to the excitement on the days before Christmas.

You will need:

a piece of thin card, at least 30 cm square.

(The back of a large cereal packet would be fine for this.)

24 empty matchboxes

paper glue

a picture to decorate the front of the calendar.

If you don't want to paint or draw something yourself, you could use a piece of wrapping paper (the type with a picture on it).

24 things to put into the matchboxes

To add to the surprise, put a mixture of different things into the boxes. Some could have sweets or chocolates and others a joke or a forfeit. (Make sure that they fit into the boxes.)

To make:

Glue the picture to the card and leave it to dry.

When it is completely stuck, turn it over, and draw round the inside tray of a matchbox 24 times leaving at least 1½ cm between each outline.

Carefully cut along the two longest sides, and from A to B.

Score along the two uncut sides of your outline, so that when you open each 'window' the flaps will bend back neatly.

Put one of the sweets or a 'surprise' onto each of the 24 spaces. Cover with a matchbox tray.

Cut along the centre of one of the broad sides of the matchbox sleeve. Bend back the flaps.

Trim the flaps to 5 mm and glue over the trays to keep them in place.

Turn the calendar over and number each window with a fibre-tipped pen from 1 to 24.

Open one window every day from the beginning of December until Christmas.

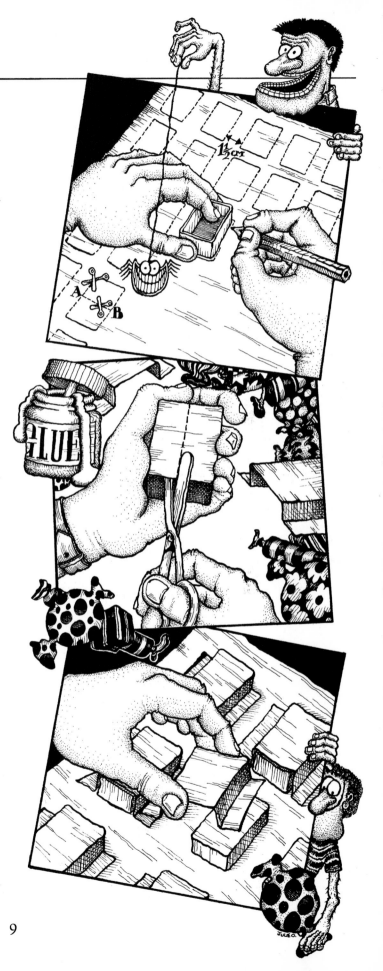

The CHRISTMAS STORY

Once, long ago in a small town called Nazareth lived a girl called Mary..

...and a boy called Joseph.

Mary and Joseph were engaged to be married...

...when one night...

AAAGH!

...an angel appeared in Mary's room. Mary was terrified at first but the angel told her not to be afraid...

...as God had chosen her for a special purpose.

You are to be the mother of God's son on earth

But I'm not married, I can't have a baby

Mary was very excited and when the angel had gone she rushed to see her cousin Elizabeth

Mary was worried that no one would believe her but Elizabeth and Zachariah were delighted.

Oh Mary that's wonderful

Elizabeth and Zachariah asked her to stay with them until the baby was born...

...but...

She's not wearing a ring

Joseph decided to marry Mary straight away

They lived happily together until one day a letter arrived ordering them to return to Bethlehem where Joseph was born.

It's from Rome, we have to go back to Bethlehem to be counted so that they can decide how much tax we have to pay.

Mary was horrified at the thought of such a long journey...

I can't go all the way to Bethlehem in my condition...

...especially on a DONKEY!

I'm sorry but it's all we have

.....but it was the law..

...and so they began their hot and dusty journey to Bethlehem.

11

Continued on page 38

Why 25 December?

There were lots of midwinter festivals long before people started to celebrate Christmas.

In the days when people worshipped the sun, the middle of winter, and particularly 21 December, which is the shortest day, were feast days.

At a time when the sun was at its weakest, people felt that it was important to make offerings and sacrifices to make sure that it returned to strength in the spring.

In Scandinavia and Norway they celebrated the winter solstice. This is the time when the sun is at its furthest from the equator. They lit Yule logs as a symbol of perpetual fire and warmth.

The Roman festival at this time was the Saturnalia. This was held in honour of their god of agriculture and was marked by feasting and drinking. Even then people practised 'Goodwill to all men' and war was banned.

The Jewish people had a festival called Hanuca, or Hanukka, in late December. This was a festival of lights, and involved the lighting of candles: one on the first day, two on the second, and so on. This festival is still celebrated by Jewish people today.

No one knows the exact date and year of the birth of Christ. The Bible does not give us any clue, and no record was handed down.

In the early days of Christianity there was no celebration of Christ's birth at all, and no special day was set aside to commemorate it.

Eventually the Church decided that it should decide on an official date. But when? The middle of winter was a good time to arrange holidays and feasts, as people were not busy working on the land because of the weather. However, the Church knew that if they arranged the celebration of Christ's Mass at this time people would still keep their old pagan traditions as well. The solution that they decided on was to allow the pagan festivals to remain, but to give them new Christian meaning.

In fact many of the things that we look on as being part of our Christmas celebrations have their origin in these earlier pagan festivities.

So December was decided upon as the month, but what date should it be?

The 25 March was the pagan festival of spring. The Church adopted this date as that of Mary's visit by the angel Gabriel, and added nine months to it to arrive at 25 December.

Christ's Mass, or Christmas as it soon became known, was first celebrated in the year 354. It was a much longer festival than we have now. It began on Christmas Eve and continued right up until 2 February, which is Candlemas day. During Cromwell's rule an act of Parliament was passed to ban all feasting and merriment and to try to abolish the celebration of Christmas. The churches were closed so that people could not worship, and those who ignored the ban were fined. This carried on for eleven years.

When Charles II became king in 1660 many of the traditions were revived, some in a slightly different form, and most not as strongly as they had been.

The Christmas that we think of as a traditional one today goes back to Victorian times. It was the Victorians who took the Christmas traditions which remained and added to them in a 'Christmas revival'.

When Christmas was moved

Up until 46 BC the new year had begun on 25 March, and was based around the phases of the moon. For all sorts of reasons this was not a very accurate method.

In 46 BC Julius Caesar revised the whole calendar, measuring it against the movement of the sun. This new calendar, called the Julian calendar, began the new year on 1 January.

As time went by, it became obvious that Caesar's astrologers had not been completely accurate, and had made the year a few minutes longer than it should have been. These extra few minutes added up over the years, and meant that the weeks and months were beginning to drift away from the seasons at which they were supposed to appear.

In 1582 Pope Gregory XIII decided that something had to be done, and a revised calendar was introduced. This was called the Gregorian Calendar.

To bring everything back to where it should be, 11 minutes 15 seconds had to be taken off the length of the year, and everything moved back by 10 days.

England didn't adopt the new calendar until the middle of the 18th century, by which time we were a full 11 days ahead of the Continent. To bring our calendar into line, 11 days were taken out of September, which meant that 25 December came 11 days earlier.

As with any major change some people objected to the new system. The country peasants in particular didn't want their festival moved to fit in with the new calendar, and continued for many years to celebrate 'Old Christmas', instead of the new date.

party invitations

Cracker card

You will need:

thin white card
paper glue
fibre-tipped pens or paints.

To make:

Transfer the template on page 16, for the cracker shape to card.

Lightly score and fold, as Fig. 1.

Paint two halves of a Christmas cracker on the two end sections.

Write your message on the next two sections.

Transfer the 'BANG' shape on page 16 to card. Cut it out and colour it.

Fold a strip of card 1 cm wide × 6 cm long backwards and forwards into a concertina shape.

Glue one end of the 'concertina' to the back of the 'BANG', and the other end to the centre panel.

Pop-up Father Christmas

You will need:

a piece of white card 280 mm × 200 mm wide
a piece of thin white card or stiff paper cut from the template on page 17
glue
crayons or fibre-tipped pens.

To make:

Fold the large piece of card in half and crease.

Colour in the picture of Father Christmas on the piece of card cut from the template.

With your picture on the outside, fold the Father Christmas in half from top to bottom.

Fold the bottom left-hand corner up to the fold and crease.

Do the same on the right hand side. Fig. 2.

Glue the back of these triangular flaps and stick into the card so that the folds align. Fig 3.

Draw or paint a snowy rooftop scene and a chimney, so that when your friends open their cards Father Christmas will pop out with his sack of presents.

Fig. 1.

Fig. 2.

Fig. 3.

Pudding card

How to make:

Using the templates on page 16, transfer the shape to folded card and cut out.

Paint the card or use scraps of cotton wool, ribbon felt, and tinsel to make a collage.

Tree card

How to make

Using the templates on page 17 transfer the 4 tree shapes to stiff paper or card and cut out.

Fold each piece in half from top to bottom.

Glue the pieces together, back to back.

FOLD

BANG

Post early for Christmas

Did you post any Christmas cards last year? Millions of people did, and millions more delivered cards by hand. In fact over a thousand million are sent annually.

The Christmas card is a recent addition to the Christmas tradition, and the very first ones to go on sale were not a great success.

The first cards were printed in 1846, and were the idea of Henry Cole, who was the first director of the Victoria and Albert Museum in London.

Only 1,000 were produced, and they were sold at Felix Summerly's Treasure House for one shilling each.

The card was a hand-coloured lithograph showing a happy family scene in the centre. In a panel on either side there were pictures of poor people being clothed and fed.

Henry Cole intended his cards to be sent by the Penny Post which had started six years earlier.

The idea was presumably not popular, and was not repeated in following years. The cards would have been quite expensive to send in large quantities. However the idea did not die completely.

A few years after Henry Cole's cards, a new colour printing process was invented.

This meant that the cards could be produced more cheaply, and as the cost reduced their popularity grew.

By 1860, the Christmas card was well established as a means of sending Christmas greetings. In 1870 the halfpenny post was introduced for cards sent in unsealed envelopes, and their popularity increased even further.

By 1880 the pressure on the postal service was enormous because of the amount of cards. The Postmaster General issued a plea which we now hear every year: 'Post early for Christmas.'

The very early cards were just illustrated visiting cards. They then became more like Valentine cards, with lace edges and flowers. Gradually the subjects changed to include snow scenes, robins, holly, mistletoe, and Father Christmas.

From the 1860s people started to collect Christmas cards and put them into albums, and probably because of this the verse began to appear inside, with just the picture on the front.

Today most people throw their cards away after Christmas. It might be a nice idea to keep your own scrapbook of your favourites.

Christmas cards

Pasta card

You will need:

dried pasta in a variety of shapes
stiff card
glue
spray paint.

To make:

Cut a piece of card to twice the finished width, score it, and carefully fold it in half.

Arrange the pasta shapes until you have a design that you like, and on a separate piece of paper make a note of where everything is so that you don't forget.

Take the pasta off the card. Go outside, put the pasta on a large piece of newspaper and spray it with paint. You will need to spray one side at a time and leave to dry between coats. Fig. 1.

When dry, rearrange the pasta on the card. Take the pieces one piece at a time, dab a small amount of glue onto the back, and stick into position.

Leave to dry and write your message inside. Fig. 2.

Thumbprint card

You will need:

thin card or stiff paper
poster paints
fibre-tip pens.

To make:

Cut a piece of card to twice the finished width, and carefully fold in half.

Tip a small amount of paint into a saucer and press your thumb into it.

On a spare piece of paper make several trial prints to remove the excess paint. Fig. 3.

When your prints look right make two, one for the body and another for the head.

Leave to dry.

With a fibre-tip pen add a nose, antlers, legs, and an eye to complete your reindeer. See page 40.

Fig. 1.

Fig. 2.

Fig. 3.

The Christmas Tree

The decorating of a tree during the midwinter festival was originally a pagan ritual, dating back to the Roman Saturnalia.

The legend that associates the fir tree with the Christian celebration of Christmas comes from Germany, and goes back to the 8th century.

'One Christmas Eve St Boniface came across an oak tree which was used by the pagan people for making human sacrifices. To prevent this ever happening again, he chopped down the tree. Miraculously in its place a fir tree sprang up. St Boniface took this to be a sign of the new faith growing up in place of the old religions.'

The people of Germany believed that the first person to have decorated a Christmas tree was Martin Luther (1483–1546). One day as he was walking through a forest he looked up at the sky which was full of stars. He was touched by the beautiful sight. He took home a small fir tree which he decorated with lighted candles, as a reminder to his followers of the heavens.

The Christmas tree was made popular in this country by Prince Albert, the husband

of Queen Victoria. Prince Albert was born in Germany where the decorated tree was already an established part of the Christmas tradition.

In 1840 he introduced a beautiful tree into the royal family's Christmas, and many other people soon followed suit.

Tinsel

The final touch to any Christmas tree is the sparkling tinsel draped from branch to branch. The story of how tinsel first came about is this:

A long time ago a poor woman was making all her preparations for Christmas. Although she had very little money, she was determined that her children would have the best Christmas that she could give them. The last thing that she had to do was to decorate the tree. She tied on the few things that she had, but the tree still looked bare. When she had done all she could, she went to bed tired and sad that despite all her efforts Christmas would not be all that she could have wished.

Overnight the spiders that lived in the house came out of their hiding-places and explored the tree. As they did so they spun their webs from branch to branch.

The Christ Child, seeing what had happened to the tree and knowing the work that had gone into its decoration, turned the webs into sparkling strands of silver.

Imagine the children's surprise and delight on Christmas morning when they found their beautiful tree.

A present from Norway

In November every year since 1947 a Norwegian spruce tree has travelled all the way from Oslo by ship and rail to Trafalgar Square in London. There it is simply decorated with white bulbs, which are ceremonially turned on.

The tree is a gift from the people of Oslo to commemorate the help which Britain gave to Norway during the 1939–45 war. The gift marks the continuing friendship which exists between our two countries.

Christmas decorations

Christmas tree decorations do not have to be complicated to look pretty. Shapes cut from stiff card and sprayed with paint or covered with glitter can be just as effective as expensive shop bought decorations.

You will need:

    stiff card
    spray paint or poster paint and a brush
    cotton
    glitter
    scissors or a craft knife
    glue

To make:

Using either the templates on page 24 or an idea of your own, trace the pattern onto the card and cut out.

Make a neat hole in the top of the shape, (a hole punch is best for this).

Paint both sides of the shape, or spread with glue and dust with glitter.

Leave to dry.

Thread cotton or ribbon through the hole and tie onto the tree.

You might like to have a theme to your Christmas tree. Here are some examples, but I am sure that you can think of many more.

Use one shape of decoration in lots of bright colours.

Have a colour theme such as red and gold, blue and white, or silver and white.

Cover the tree with empty matchboxes wrapped in coloured wrapping-paper and tied onto the tree with ribbon.

Tie sweets covered in shiny paper onto your tree. (This has the advantage that after Christmas you can eat the decorations.)

Decorated baubles

Plain coloured baubles can be made even more attractive by painting on a pattern with glue and dusting with glitter, or sticking on scraps of lace and beads, as you can see in the picture opposite.

23

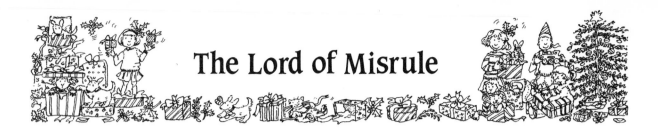

The Lord of Misrule

Since Roman times the midwinter celebrations have involved a topsy-turvy changing of roles. The Roman masters would change places with their slaves, and the slaves could say and do what they liked until the end of the festival.

In medieval times the Church appointed a 'boy bishop'. The chosen boy, usually a choirboy, was for the duration of the holiday treated exactly as the real bishop would be. He wore the bishop's robes, headed a procession in his honour, and preached sermons. The only thing that he was not allowed to do was to celebrate mass.

From the Middle Ages up until the custom was banned under the Puritans, a 'Lord of Misrule' was appointed at the court and in the large private houses to preside over the festivities.

It was this person's job to make sure that the merrymaking did not stop, and to devise all sorts of sports and entertainments to keep people amused. These revels often got out of hand and ended in chaos.

In 1418 the Corporation of London banned the practice of disguise except in people's homes. This was because of the increase in crime over the Christmas period when people's identity was masked and they could not be recognized.

This change of roles and disguise still continues in the theatre over Christmas when in pantomime a girl takes the part of the principal boy, and a man the dame.

HOW TO MAKE
Saint Nicholas letters

In Holland these biscuits are made and eaten on 6 December, which is Saint Nicholas' day.

You will need:

8 oz (225g) of frozen shortcrust pastry
4 oz (100g) of marzipan
a small amount of milk in a saucer.

To make:

Leave the pastry out of the fridge overnight to defrost.

Roll out the pastry to about as thick as a 50 pence piece.

Cut the pastry into strips 10 cm long and 5 cm wide.

Roll the marzipan into a long sausage the width of a pencil.

Cut the 'sausage' into lengths slightly shorter than your pastry strips.

Put one 'sausage' of marzipan onto each pastry strip.

Dip your finger in the milk. (Make sure it's clean first!)

Spread a little of the milk round the edges of the pastry and roll it up, pressing the edges to stop the marzipan oozing out when you cook them.

Make up letters with the pastry and marzipan mixture. If you have to use two strips to make letters like 'K', brush a little milk on the edges that you want to join before you push them together. If you have to lengthen or shorten any of the pieces, make sure that you reseal the ends.

Lightly grease a baking tray with a little butter or lard.

Put the letters on the baking sheet 2 cm apart.

Bake them at Gas mark 7, Reg 425°F, for 10–15 minutes.

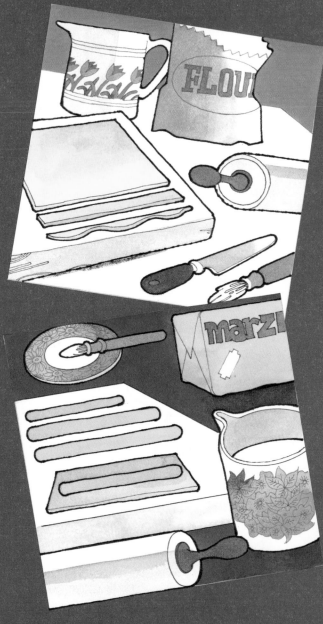

Christmas Eve, and twelve of the clock.
'Now they are all on their knees,'
An elder said as we sat in a flock,
By the embers in fireside ease.

We pictured the meek mild creatures, where
They dwelt in their strawy pen,
Nor did it occur to one of us there
To doubt they were kneeling then.

So fair a fancy few would weave
In these years! Yet I feel
If someone said, on Christmas Eve,
'Come; see the oxen kneel

'In the lonely barton by yonder coomb,
Our children used to know,'
I should go with him in the gloom,
Hoping it might be so.

Thomas Hardy

A magical time

Because people believed that Jesus was born at midnight on Christmas Eve, it was considered to be a magical and mysterious time, and there are many traditions and superstitions connected with it.

As the baby Jesus was born in a stable surrounded by animals, it is not surprising that some of these beliefs were about things that happened to people's own animals at this time.

It was thought that cattle and sheep in the fields and wild animals of the forest knelt down in prayer at twelve o'clock to worship the new baby.

Bees were supposed to wake from their winter hibernation to 'buzz' a song of praise, and animals of all kinds were supposed to be able to talk for a few moments.

To see all these amazing things it was necessary to have led a completely blameless life. As no one could claim to be perfect, it was difficult to prove or disprove the legend.

In the past when people were more afraid of ghosts than we are today, midnight on Christmas Eve was thought to be a time when 'Ghosts, Witches, and things like that' had no power to harm them. Perhaps that is why people felt safe to sit around the fire telling each other ghost stories, believing that no harm could come to them . . . at least not until the next day.

In Ireland there was a belief that the gates of paradise were opened at twelve o'clock to welcome in the souls of anyone who died at that time.

Dumb cakes

Dumb cakes were baked on Christmas Eve by girls who wanted to find out who they were going to marry.

First the girl would fast all day. Then in complete silence she would bake the cake which was a mixture of barley, salt, and wheatmeal. When it was cooked she would prick her initials in the top of the cake, place it by the fireside, open the front door and wait for midnight.

At the last stroke of midnight her future husband was supposed to walk in and leave his initials next to hers.

Afterwards she would eat the cake, though it couldn't have been very appetizing.

Christmas Eve would also have been the time when the Yule log was ceremonially dragged back to the house and lit.

In this country we celebrate the Eve of Christmas by hanging up our stockings ready to be filled with presents by Father Christmas, and going to the midnight church services which are held at churches all over the country.

In other countries a special meal is eaten and sometimes presents are exchanged.

Father Christmas

The character of Father Christmas, has his base in both Christian and Pagan tradition.

The Christian origins are from a 4th century saint called Nicholas who was the Archbishop of Lycia.

Many stories surround this particular saint, all of which associate him with children in one way or another.

In one legend he is claimed to have been staying at an inn where the murder of three children had been committed. In a dream he learned of the murder and found the bodies of the children in a brine tub. He brought them back to life and after extracting a confession from the innkeeper, he then converted him to Christianity.

Another story is that Saint Nicholas gave a present of gold to three poor girls to allow them to marry. This was in the days when a girl's parents had to provide a dowry (a sum of money) in order that their daughter could find a husband.

The story goes that Saint Nicholas threw the three bags of gold in through an open window. They landed in the girls' stockings which were hanging up to dry in front of the fire. This is thought to have led to the custom of hanging up stockings on Christmas Eve, in anticipation of them being filled with presents.

There are also stories which tell of Saint Nicholas feeding hungry children.

Because of these legends he was made patron saint of children. His saint's day, which is on 6 December, is celebrated in many countries by giving gifts to children.

The pagan traditions of Father Christmas go back to both the Roman and the Norse people. The Norsemen believed that it was their god Woden who brought them presents at his mid-winter festival.

When Christianity swept through Britain the custom still continued, so the Church let it carry on but changed it slightly so that the person bringing the gifts was Saint Nicholas.

Under the Puritans' rule saints were not recognized as such and Saint Nicholas became Father Christmas. This was a cross between the saint and a character from a traditional mummers' play, acted out at around Christmas time. This Father Christmas was portrayed as wearing a crown of holly leaves, and a grey beard.

The Father Christmas that appears on cards and in department stores is the most popular version and originated in America.

An American called Thomas Nast drew a picture of Father Christmas for 'Harpers' magazine in the 1860s. This showed him as a jolly old man with a long white beard wearing red robes, trimmed with white fur.

The nineteenth-century Dutch settlers in America called Father Christmas Sinter Klaass, which is Dutch for Saint Nicholas. The Americans adopted the expression but pronounced it Santa Claus.

Santa Claus is the name of a town in America. In its park there is a statue of Saint Nicholas twenty-three feet high. There is also a post office which deals with all the letters which are posted in America addressed to him.

a Christmas stocking

You will need:

2 pieces of felt 230 mm square
fabric glue
scraps of cotton wool or tinsel to decorate.

To Make:

Trace the template and cut out two stocking shapes.

Cut a strip 20 mm wide and 200 mm long to hang the stocking up by.

Spread glue around 5 mm of the outer edge of the stocking, leaving the top edge free.

Stick the two sections together and leave to dry completely.

Fold down 30 mm of the top to make a collar.

Fold the hanging strip into two and glue it inside the back of the stocking.

Decorate the stocking with tinsel or cotton wool to make a 'fur' edge.

If you wish to fill your stocking with presents, then you will need to stitch the edges together. You can do this either with oversewing or using blanket stitch as shown.

If you would like to make this stocking shape larger or smaller, draw a grid behind the template, and then draw another grid but making the squares either larger or smaller.

Copy the contents of each square exactly onto your new grid.

You can use this method to enlarge or reduce any of the templates in this book.

Yuletide

The festival of Yule was celebrated by the Norse people at the time of the winter solstice (when the sun was at its furthest from the equator) on 21 December.

The Yule log was burnt as a symbol of perpetual fire which they believed to be sacred.

This ancient custom led to the tradition of burning a large log at Christmas time. The log had to be lit from the remains of the previous year's log as a symbol of the warmth and light which would return in the spring.

Yule logs were chosen with great care, and dragged ceremonially back to the house, often with the younger children riding astride it. It was kept alight for the whole twelve days of Christmas, so it had to be enormous.

It was considered to be very bad luck to allow the fire to go out and even worse to relight it from a neighbour's. Because of this, bonfires were often kept alight in the villages at Christmas time (matches had not been invented then).

Although we do not burn Yule logs any more we do sometimes eat them at Christmas (the chocolate version!)

A chocolate log

You will need:

2 bought Swiss rolls
4 oz (100g) butter
8 oz (225g) icing sugar (sifted)
2 tsp cocoa powder
1 tbsp milk.

To make:

Beat the butter with half the icing sugar until smooth.

In another bowl mix the cocoa powder with 2 tablespoons of boiling water.

Leave the cocoa mixture to cool, and add it to the butter and icing sugar.

Add the rest of the icing sugar and mix it all together well.

Cut one of the Swiss rolls in half at an angle. (You don't need the other half, so you can eat it if you like.)

With a little of the icing, stick the short piece to the other Swiss roll, to look like a branch.

Cover the whole log with icing.

Make swirls in the icing to make it look like bark.

To finish off your log you could add a plastic robin, or some artificial ivy leaves.

Ice

When Winter scourged the meadow and the hill
And in the withered leafage worked his will,
The water shrank, and shuddered and stood still, —
Then built himself a magic house of glass,
Irised with memories of flowers and grass,
Wherein to sit and watch the fury pass.

Charles G D Roberts

I've asked a great many people,
  But nobody seems to know,
How the pirates kept their Christmas
  In the days of long ago;

How many loaded galleons
  On Christmas Day they sank,
And how many merchant seamen
  They made to walk the plank;

Or whether they chanted carols
  As round the decks they rolled,
And made each other presents
  Out of their hoards of gold;

And covered a mast with green leaves
  And called it a Christmas-tree,
And hung it with shining sequins
  On the shore of a tropical sea;

And lit the rum round the pudding
  And cursed in a kindly way,
But refused to do any business
  Because it was Christmas Day.

I've asked a great many people,
  But nobody seems to know,
How the pirates kept their Christmas
  In the days of long ago.

E.V. Knox

The First Noel

In the month before Christmas everywhere you go there are carols playing. In shopping centres there are bands playing for charity, and the radio and television play the old familiar tunes over and over again.

The word 'carol' means 'ring dance'. These were songs sung at religious festivals, at any time of the year and not only Christmas.

Over a period of many years the singing of carols almost completely died out. A few people tried unsuccessfully to revive the custom but perhaps the tunes or words had lost their popular appeal.

In 1871 the organist of Magdalen College Oxford, and a fellow of the same college compiled a book called *Christmas Carols, Old and New*. As the title suggests, it contained the traditional carols which had survived, plus a great many new ones.

All the carols in the book were easy to play and sing, and by the end of the nineteenth century the carol was once more popular.

Most of the carols that we sing today date from this time.

The carol 'Silent Night', was written by Father Joseph Mohr, a parish priest at the church of Oberndorf in Austria. The music was written by Franz Xaver Gruber, the organist at the same church.

One Christmas Eve the priest and the organist went to the church to practise on the organ. To their horror, they realized that the mice had eaten through the bellows, and they would not work.

Not to be defeated, the priest showed the organist a new carol which he had written. The organist quickly rescored it, and on Christmas Day 1818 'Silent Night' was first performed to the accompaniment of a guitar.

Waits

The 'Waits' were originally the town watch, who patrolled the streets calling the hour of the night and seeing that all was well (in the days before policemen and bedside clocks).

The term was later used to describe musicians who walked round the town at Christmas time playing, and collecting money, and also to groups of professional actors who toured the country giving performances in private houses.

The tradition of the waits led to the practice of singing carols from door to door.

36

Carolling around the estate

The six of us met at Alan's house
    and Jane brought a carol sheet
that she got free from the butcher's shop
    when she bought the Sunday meat.

Jeremy had a new lantern light
    made by his Uncle Ted
and Jim had 'borrowed' his Dad's new torch
    which flashed white, green and red.

Our first call was at Stew Foster's place
    where we sang 'Three Kings' real well.
But his mother couldn't stand the row
    and she really gave us hell!

We drifted on from door to door
    singing carols by lantern light.
Jane's lips were purple with the cold;
    my fingers were turning white.

Around nine we reached the chippie shop
    where we ordered pie and peas,
and with hot grease running down our hands
    we started to defreeze.

I reached home tired out, but my mum said,
    'Your cousin Anne's been here.
She's carolling tomorrow night
    and I said you'd go, my dear.'

Wes Magee

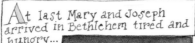

At last Mary and Joseph arrived in Bethlehem tired and hungry...

Only to find..

BETHLEHEM HILTON

...everywhere full.

I'm sorry, we're full, try the one down the street

Sorry — nothing left

At last a friendly innkeeper took pity on them and offered them the use of his stable for the night

And during the night Mary's baby was born

39

Continued on page 50

Reindeer

It was in 1832 with the publication of Clement Clarke Moore's poem 'A Visit from St. Nicholas' that the reindeer became part of popular Christmas tradition.

It was this poem which gave the reindeer their names of Dasher, Dancer, Prancer, Vixen, Comet, Cupid, Donner, and Blitzen.

Rudolf was not amongst the original team. His appearance came later in 1939 when a song was published about his glowing nose.

Reindeer live in the Arctic. They are very strong, extremely sure-footed on ice, and are used to pull heavy loads. This is perhaps why they became connected with pulling Father Christmas's sleigh, full to the brim with toys all the way from the North Pole.

There are no legends to my knowledge that connect reindeer with the ability to fly. None of the pictures drawn of them show them with wings of any kind. Let's just put it down to part of the Christmas magic.

What the donkey saw

No room in the inn, of course,
And not that much in the stable,
What with the shepherds, Magi, Mary,
Joseph, the heavenly host —
Not to mention the baby
Using our manger as a cot.
You couldn't have squeezed another cherub in
For love or money.

Still, in spite of the overcrowding,
I did my best to make them feel wanted.
I could see the baby and I
Would be going places together.

U.A. Fanthorpe

The snowman

I built him with laughter
   And warm winter smiles.
I built him so tall
   You can see him for miles,
And at night the starlight
   Makes him glint like a king,
And the moonbeams dance round
   As the winter winds sing.

I built him with joy
   For Christmas is here.
He's my champion my trophy,
   My prize for the year.
And the glow from the snow
   Paints him silvery bright,
And my king among snowmen
   Glistens snow white.

But spring holds his future
   For winter won't last,
And my snowman will melt
   To a thing of the past.
But each year for ever
   His memory will bring
A crown for his throne
   With the snowdrops of spring.

Lynn Zirkel

A visit from Saint Nicholas

This lovely Christmas poem would be perfect to read out loud on Christmas Eve. You could perhaps divide the poem into parts and read a section each.

Use the instructions around the poem to help you perfect your performance, and read the poem out loud a few times to get the feel of it.

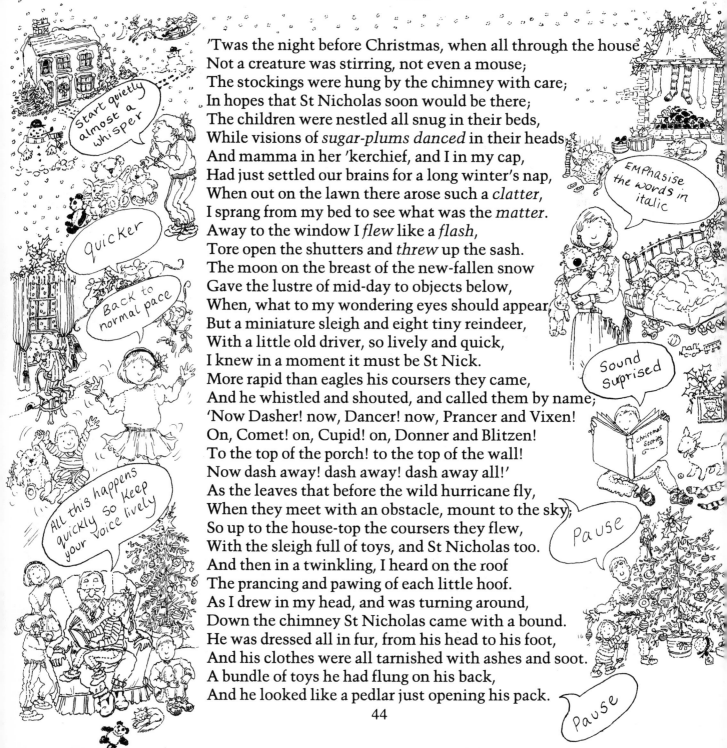

'Twas the night before Christmas, when all through the house
Not a creature was stirring, not even a mouse;
The stockings were hung by the chimney with care,
In hopes that St Nicholas soon would be there;
The children were nestled all snug in their beds,
While visions of *sugar-plums danced* in their heads;
And mamma in her 'kerchief, and I in my cap,
Had just settled our brains for a long winter's nap,
When out on the lawn there arose such a *clatter*,
I sprang from my bed to see what was the *matter*.
Away to the window I *flew* like a *flash*,
Tore open the shutters and *threw* up the sash.
The moon on the breast of the new-fallen snow
Gave the lustre of mid-day to objects below,
When, what to my wondering eyes should appear,
But a miniature sleigh and eight tiny reindeer,
With a little old driver, so lively and quick,
I knew in a moment it must be St Nick.
More rapid than eagles his coursers they came,
And he whistled and shouted, and called them by name;
'Now Dasher! now, Dancer! now, Prancer and Vixen!
On, Comet! on, Cupid! on, Donner and Blitzen!
To the top of the porch! to the top of the wall!
Now dash away! dash away! dash away all!'
As the leaves that before the wild hurricane fly,
When they meet with an obstacle, mount to the sky;
So up to the house-top the coursers they flew,
With the sleigh full of toys, and St Nicholas too.
And then in a twinkling, I heard on the roof
The prancing and pawing of each little hoof.
As I drew in my head, and was turning around,
Down the chimney St Nicholas came with a bound.
He was dressed all in fur, from his head to his foot,
And his clothes were all tarnished with ashes and soot.
A bundle of toys he had flung on his back,
And he looked like a pedlar just opening his pack.

Start quietly almost a whisper

Quicker

Back to normal pace

All this happens quickly so keep your voice lively

Emphasise the words in italic

Sound Surprised

Pause

Pause

44

His eyes — how they twinkled! his dimples how merry!
His cheeks were like roses, his nose like a cherry!
His droll little mouth was drawn up like a bow,
And the beard of his chin was as white as the snow;
The stump of a pipe he held tight in his teeth,
And the smoke it encircled his head like a wreath;
He had a broad face and a little round belly,
That shook when he laughed, like a bowlful of jelly.
He was chubby and plump, a right jolly old elf,
And I laughed when I saw him, in spite of myself;
A wink of his eye and a twist of his head,
Soon gave me to know I had nothing to dread.
He spoke not a word, but went straight to his work,
And filled all the stockings; then turned with a jerk,
And laying his finger aside of his nose,
And giving a nod, up the chimney he rose;
He sprang to his sleigh, to his team gave a whistle,
And away they all flew like the down of a thistle.
But I heard him exclaim, 'ere he drove out of sight,
'Happy Christmas to all, and to all a good night.'

Clement Clarke Moore

You could add to the atmosphere of your poetry reading by setting an armchair aside (or more than one if you are reading it with friends) and perhaps reading by the light of a lamp while turning out the main lights.

Before people had televisions they would often get together to sing and read out poems aloud.

You could use some of the other pieces of poetry in this book to make an evening of Christmas poetry. Or you could ask your family and friends a few days before Christmas to find their favourite Christmas poem or piece of prose to read on Christmas Eve.

If you wish to be more adventurous still, you could extend your production to include songs as well as poetry. This is more difficult, though, unless you have someone who can play a musical instrument to accompany you.

Robins

Every year millions of Christmas cards are sold with pictures of robins on the front.

When the Penny Post was introduced in 1840, the postmen wore bright red uniforms, and early cards often showed the robin with a card in its beak as 'a robin postman'.

Because the robin chooses its mate in December his plumage is at its best when most birds are looking rather dull. This, combined with the fact that robins do not share most birds' fear of people, makes them very noticeable in the garden during the winter months.

There are various legends as to how the robin got his beautiful red plumage. The most popular one is that the robin was present in the stable when Jesus was born. Joseph had to go out to find wood for the fire as it was dying down.

He was gone for a long time and Mary was worried that the fire would go out and the baby would get cold.

Down flew some small birds and fanned the dying embers of the fire back to life.

Whilst doing this the feathers on their breasts got singed. Mary was so grateful that she turned the feathers to a beautiful red as a reminder of their kindness.

It is rather strange that the robin should be associated with the season of good will, for although it is friendly towards humans it can be quite vicious to other birds.

Robin's song

Robins sang in England,
   Frost or rain or snow,
All the long December days
   Endless years ago.

Robins sang in England
   Before the Legions came,
Before our English fields were tilled
   Or England was a name.

Robins sang in England
   When forests dark and wild
Stretched across from sea to sea
   And Jesus was a child.

Listen! In the frosty dawn
   From his leafless bough
The same brave song he ever sang
   A robin's singing now.

Rodney Bennett

A Christmas Carol

Before the paling of the stars,
  Before the winter morn
  Before the earliest cockcrow
  Jesus Christ was born;
    Born in a stable,
  Cradled in a manger,
In the world His hands had made
    Born a stranger.

Priest and king lay fast asleep
  In Jerusalem
Young and old lay fast asleep
  In crowded Bethlehem;
Saint and Angel, ox and ass,
  Kept a watch together,
  Before the Christmas daybreak
  In the winter weather.

Jesus on His Mother's breast,
  In the stable cold,
Spotless Lamb of God was he,
  Shepherd of the fold:
Let us kneel with Mary Maid,
  With Joseph bent and hoary,
  With Saint and Angel, ox and ass,
  To hail the King of glory.

Christina Rossetti

Christmas disasters

Mary and Joseph decided to stay in Bethlehem until Mary was fit enough to travel

They named the baby, Jesus, as the angel had told them.

In the sky above the house in which they were living a bright star had appeared

Three wise men who studied astronomy noticed this new bright star and set out to follow it.

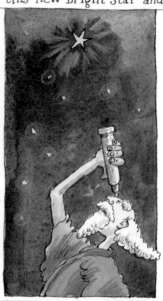

....until eventually they met at King Herod's palace.

From their own lands they travelled on and on......

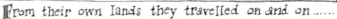

51

Continued on page 82

Evergreens

Evergreens have been part of the mid-winter celebrations since long before the Christmas festival. They played a very symbolic part because they stay green and alive when all other plants look dead and bare. They were seen as representing everlasting life and hope for the return of spring.

Mistletoe

Mistletoe is a parasitic plant. It has no roots of its own and lives off the tree that it attaches itself to — without that tree it would die.

Mistletoe grows mainly on apple trees but occasionally is found on ash trees. Very rarely it is found on oak trees, and because the oak was a sacred tree to the druids they believed that the mistletoe which grew on it had all sorts of magical properties.

They cut the mistletoe with a golden sickle (a type of curved knife) and used it to protect themselves from witches, to cure illness, and to ensure peace and prosperity.

The tradition of kissing under the mistletoe may have its origins in the druid belief that mistletoe was a symbol of fertility.

Nowadays people hang up a kissing ring or bush in their houses. Girls who receive a kiss under the mistletoe are supposed to remove a berry, until no more berries remain and then no more kisses may be claimed.

Pick a berry of mistletoe
For every kiss that's given
When the berries have all gone
There's an end to kissing.

Because of its associations with pagan ceremonies and particularly with rituals involving sacrifice, both human and animal, mistletoe is rarely used in church decorations.

A Norse legend which is retold on page 124 recounts how Baldur who was one of the gods, was killed by a sprig of mistletoe.

Rosemary

This sweet-smelling herb is not used so much at Christmas now. It was probably more popular before air-fresheners were invented as its fragrance would make a room smell lovely.

According to legend the fragrance was given to it when Mary used it to hang Jesus's clothes on while they dried.

The holly and the ivy

These two plants were used in pre-Christian times to represent male and female, the holly being the male and the ivy the female.

The Christians gave the holly a new meaning as its sharp pointed leaves and bright red berries symbolized Christ's crown of thorns, with the berries being drops of blood.

The Glastonbury thorn

Soon after Christ's death, Joseph of Arimathea came to Britain to spread the Christian message. The legend of the thorn is that it was originally Joseph's staff, which he had brought from the Holy Land. It was thought that while he lay down to rest he had pushed the staff into the ground beside him. When he awoke the staff had taken root and begun to grow and blossom. He left it there and it flowered every Christmas as well as every spring.

A Puritan tried to cut down the tree and is said to have been blinded by a splinter of the wood before he could do so.

The original thorn did eventually die but not before many cuttings had been taken. It is one of these cuttings which is in the grounds of Glastonbury Abbey today.

HOW TO MAKE
a kissing bunch

You will need:

2 wire coat-hangers (the thin sort that you get from the cleaners)
evergreens, such as holly, yew, laurel or ivy.
a bunch of mistletoe
a reel of florist's wire. Ordinary wire is not bendy enough, although fuse wire would be all right.
ribbon.

To make:

Bend the coat-hangers into two circles.

Tie them firmly together at the top and bottom, at right angles to each other.

Bend the hook of one hanger so that both hooks face the same way.

Using florist's wire tie the greenery to the coat-hangers until you can't see any bits of coat-hanger showing through.

Tie the mistletoe to the bottom of the ring with the ribbon.

Hang your finished kissing bunch from the ceiling, and wait!

53

HOW TO MAKE
a Christmas bough

You will need:

a branch (try to find one which is an interesting
   shape)
a can of spray paint or artificial snow
a heavy flower pot
some stones

To make:

Dust any loose pieces of bark from the bough.

Go outside and spray the bough with artificial snow
or paint.

Leave to dry.

Put the branch into a flowerpot
and pack the stones
around it to keep it upright.

Carefully decorate your bough.

A Christmas feast

Now that the time has come wherein
Our Saviour Christ was born,
The larder's full of beef and pork,
The granary's full of corn,
As God hath plenty to thee sent,
Take comfort of thy labours,
And let it never thee repent
To feed thy needy neighbours.

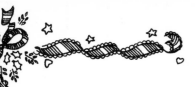

Festive fare

Food and feasting have always been an important part of the Christmas tradition. Rich and poor alike would try to celebrate by eating and drinking something which they would not normally have during the rest of the year. At the time when most people worked for a Lord of the manor it was customary for him to provide or at least contribute to the meal. For the ordinary worker this would probably consist of chicken or goose cooked in the local baker's oven, and a jug of ale; the rich, on the other hand, would banquet on such delicacies as swan and peacock.

The Christmas bird

Although we now associate turkey with our traditional Christmas dinner, the goose was the bird most commonly eaten at Christmas for three hundred years or so.

When Queen Elizabeth I first heard the news of the defeat of the Spanish Armada, on Christmas Eve 1588, she was dining on goose. She decreed that goose should be eaten at Christmas from then on.

Theories differ as to how the turkey got to this country, but one thing is certain — it did not come from Turkey! It did in fact come from America, and was imported here in the early sixteenth century when they began to breed them in large quantities.

King Henry VIII is the first person that we know from records who ate turkey on Christmas day, and presumably made it popular.

In the eighteenth century two peers decided to race a flock of geese and a flock of turkeys from Norfolk to London to market. The turkeys should have won easily as they were by far the fastest, but the geese overtook them because they could eat as they walked and did not stop to sleep at night.

Christmas pie

Christmas pie was a forerunner of mince pie and contained a meat and fruit mixture. This is what the old nursery rhyme was referring to:

> *Little Jack Horner*
> *Sat in a corner*
> *Eating a Christmas pie*
>
> *He put in his thumb*
> *And pulled out a plum*
> *And said what a good boy am I.*

The rhyme is not referring to any ordinary pie, though. At the time when Henry VIII was trying to take all the power away from the monasteries, Jack Horner was steward to the abbot of Glastonbury. The abbot knew that eventually Henry would take their land and properties away, and to try to prevent this he devised a plan. He took the title deeds to twelve of the richest manors belonging to the abbey and had them baked under the crust of a pie. He gave this to his steward and told him to take it to the king.

On the way to London Jack is said to have discovered the secret of the pie and taken out the title deeds to the richest property there, that of the Manor of Mells in Somerset. The abbot's plan did not work and all the lands and property belonging to Glastonbury Abbey were confiscated. But Jack kept his house, where we presume he lived happily to the end of his days.

HOW TO MAKE
some Christmas food

During the cold winter evenings mulled wine or ale was often served. Why not try this non-alcoholic version for your party?

You will need:

1 orange
6 cloves
2 bottles of ginger beer
1 cinnamon stick.

To make:

Push the cloves into the orange and bake it in the oven for half an hour (Gas mark 4 Reg 450°F).

Cut the orange into slices and put these into a pan with the ginger beer.

Bring the liquid almost to the boil.

Leave to cool slightly and pour into glasses.

N.B. If the liquid is too hot when you pour it into the glasses, they may crack. To prevent this, put a cold teaspoon into each glass when you fill it.

To serve the punch, try frosting the glasses as shown in the photograph. Decorated glasses make even a glass of lemonade look extra special.

To frost glasses

You will need:

the white of an egg
caster sugar
a small paintbrush.

To make:

Beat the egg white until frothy.

Paint onto the glasses any pattern you like. Fig. 1.

Put the caster sugar on a plate and roll the glass in it. The sugar will stick to the part which you have painted and show up your design. Fig. 2.

Pour a little of the remaining egg-white into a saucer and dip the rim of the glass into it.

Dip the rim into a saucer of caster sugar.

Leave to dry for a few hours before you use.

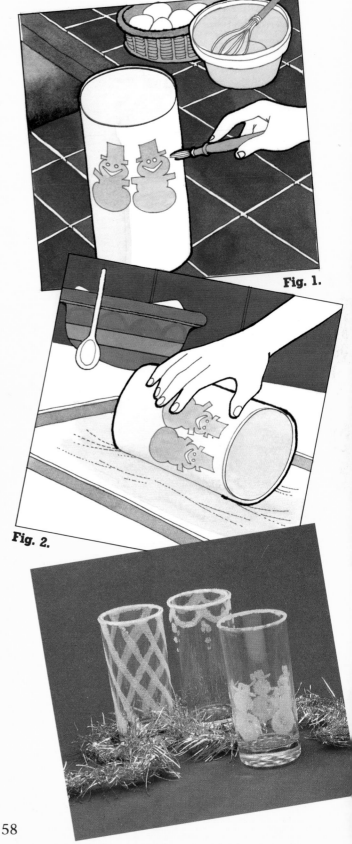

Fig. 1.

Fig. 2.

Christmas pudding sweets

Why not make some of these delicious sweets to give to your friends as presents? They are a bit fiddly to make but are well worth the effort.

You will need:

¼ lb (100g) plain chocolate
2 oz (50g) butter
1 tablespoon orange juice
finely grated rind of an orange
yolk of 2 eggs
1 oz (25g) ground almonds
1 oz (25g) cake crumbs
¼ lb (100g) icing sugar
chocolate strands.

To make:

Break the chocolate into pieces and put into a basin with the butter.

Put the basin on top of a pan of hot water, and leave until the chocolate and butter have both melted. Use a very gentle heat to do this, otherwise the chocolate will overcook and become lumpy.

Take off the heat. Add the egg yolks and mix well.

Add everything else except the chocolate strands and mix it all together.

Leave the mixture in a cool place for 2 hours.

Roll the mixture into a long sausage, and cut into 30 equal pieces.

Roll each piece into a ball, and then roll it in the chocolate strands.

To decorate you will need:

¼ lb (100g) icing sugar
a small amount of marzipan
green and red food colouring
the white of an egg.

Beat the egg-white until frothy.

Gradually beat the egg-white into the icing sugar until the mixture forms a stiff paste.

On a board dusted with icing sugar, take small balls of the mixture and flatten into irregular shapes as shown.

Lay one of these pieces over each sweet.

Work a little red food colouring into one portion of the marzipan and a little green into another. Cut out holly leaf shapes from the green marzipan and roll the red into small balls to form berries.

Decorate your sweets and put them into paper cases.

Mince pies

The mincemeat with which we fill our mince pies began like Christmas pudding as a mixture of meats and fruit. This was baked into an oblong crust which represented the Crib, and on top was baked a pastry child. At the time of the Reformation the Puritans forbad the eating of mince pies, because of their religious connections. When mince pies became popular again in the reign of Charles II the shape had changed to round and the child was no longer used as decoration.

These early pies were eaten at the start of a meal.

Two superstitions which surround the eating of mince pies are 'He who eats twelve mince pies in twelve houses over Christmas will have twelve happy months' and 'Whoever eats a mince pie every day from Christmas to Twelfth night will have twelve happy months'. The custom is also to make a wish on the first bite of your first pie. Who knows if any of these superstitions work? Just eat a lot of mince pies to be on the safe side!

'Plum pudding'

Christmas pudding, or plum pudding as it is sometimes known, started out its history as a thick savoury porridge made with beef, veal, wine, sherry, lemon and orange juice, sugar, raisins, currants, cinnamon, cloves, and prunes, which are dried plums, hence the name 'plum porridge' The whole sticky mixture was thickened with brown bread

and eaten with a spoon. It was not unusual in the past to find meat and fruit mixed together in this way as the fruit helped to preserve the keeping qualities of the meat. Eventually the meat was left out of the mixture, and suet was included to thicken it to the consistency that we are familiar with today.

The early puddings were round in shape. This was because they were boiled in a cloth, quite often in the copper used for boiling the washing, but not at the same time! As the fruit swelled during the cooking, the puddings became round. The only reason that our puddings are a different shape is that we cook them in basins, which is a much less messy way of doing it.

Traditionally Christmas puddings were made on the last Sunday before Advent commonly known as 'Stir up Sunday'. This name came about not because of the stirring of the pudding but because a special prayer for that Sunday in the book of Common Prayer begins with the line 'Stir up we beseech thee, O Lord . . .'

One tradition which does seem to be dying out is that of hiding coins in the pudding. Originally the Christmas pudding would be stirred by each member of the family in turn. They would all make a wish, and then into the mixture would go a coin, a ring, and a thimble. The coin was for wealth, the ring for a marriage, and the thimble for a life of blessedness.

The popularity of soaking the pudding in spirit and setting fire to it has not reduced and does make the pudding look very dramatic as it is carried to the table, that is if the flames do not go out on the way.

some edible presents

Home made sweets make lovely presents, especially if you pack them in boxes covered in Christmas paper and put clear film over them to keep them fresh.

Chocolate pineapple

You will need:

a small tin of pineapple rings, or some glacé pineapple
a large bar of chocolate.

To make:

If you are using tinned pineapple put it into a sieve, over a basin, and leave until **thoroughly** drained (otherwise the chocolate will not stick to it).

Melt the chocolate over a pan of hot, but not boiling water.

Cut each of the rings into 8 pieces.

Using a skewer, dip the pieces into the chocolate until they are covered.

Leave to set on greaseproof paper.

You can also follow this method to cover dates or brazil nuts, but remember to take the stones out of the dates first. You can fill the hole left by the stone with marzipan if you like.

Peppermint snowmen

You will need:

8 oz (225g) icing sugar
1 egg-white
a few drops of peppermint essence
blue or black food colouring
a piece of black paper for hats
a small amount of marzipan for scarves.

To make:

Beat the egg-white until frothy.

Sieve the icing sugar into a basin.

Add the icing sugar to the egg-white until it makes a stiff paste.

Add the peppermint essence and mix well.

Roll out the mixture to ¼″ thick.

Cut circles 1″ across for the body and the same number of slightly smaller ones for the head.

Push a large and a small circle together to form the snowman shape.

Colour a small amount of the leftover icing blue or black, and make small balls of it for eyes and buttons.

If you wish, you can finish off the snowmen with hats cut from black paper or card, and scarves made from marzipan.

Leave your finished sweets to dry overnight.

Holly biscuits

You will need:

½ lb (225g) self-raising flour
1½ level teaspoons cinnamon
a pinch of salt
5 oz (150g) butter
¼ lb (100g) castor sugar
beaten egg to mix.

To make:

Sift the flour, salt and cinnamon together in a basin.

Rub in the butter, until it looks like breadcrumbs. Add the sugar and mix.

Mix to a stiff dough with the egg. Knead.

Put the mixture into a polythene bag and leave it in the fridge for 30 minutes.

Roll out to ¼″ deep and cut into 36 holly leaves. You can do this either with a biscuit-cutter or a glass. Place on a baking tray brushed with oil and bake at Gas mark 4, Reg 350°F for 12–15 mins.

To decorate you will need:

8 oz (225g) icing sugar
a few drops of green food colouring
marzipan and red food colouring for the berries.
a small paintbrush

Mix the icing sugar and water together to make a fairly stiff paste.

Colour with green food colouring, and spread onto the biscuits (when they have cooled).

Paint the veins of the leaves with a brush dipped into the green colouring. If you want to add berries, do so by using balls of marzipan coloured red.

Mummers

Masked performances called mummers' plays, were once found in almost every village in England, and some still survive.

All the plays follow the same theme, although the words and characters vary from place to place.

The theme of the play is the triumph of spring over winter. A character is killed early in the play to represent the crops dying in the winter. In the spring as the crops grow again, the dead man is revived by the doctor.

The hero of most of the plays was St. George but the villain varied from place to place, and often a real person's name was used.

The plays were performed in private houses, and were considered to bring good luck to the occupants of the house. This luck was broken if the players were recognized, so they wore masks, blackened their faces and disguised their voices.

The dialogue of the mummers' plays that remain today is difficult to understand. One explanation of this is that the lines were passed on from father to son by word of mouth, rather than the plays being written down. As presumably people only knew their own parts and the lines just before and after them, all sorts of mix-ups could have occurred.

There was a version of the mummers' play which was acted out at court and called a 'masque'. The disguises for these were elaborate and very costly.

The Puritans banned the performance of both the masque and the mummers' plays, and when Charles II became king neither was revived. The masque probably because it would have cost too much, and the mummers' plays perhaps because no one could remember the words.

Two places where the mummers' plays are still performed on Boxing Day, are Marshfield near Bristol, and Crookham in Hampshire.

In Marshfield the players wear costumes made completely from strips of paper, and are called the 'paper boys'.

In Crookham the costumes are a mixture of wallpaper strips similar to the paper boys, and more 'normal' dress such as a Father Christmas costume, and top hat and tails for the doctor.

The sixth day of Christmas
My true love sent to me
Six geese a-laying,
Five gold rings,
Four colly birds,
Three French hens,
Two turtle doves
And a partridge in a pear tree.

The seventh day of Christmas
My true love sent to me
Seven swans a-swimming,
Six geese a-laying,
Five gold rings,
Four colly birds,
Three French hens,
Two turtle doves
And a partridge in a pear tree.

The eighth day of Christmas
My true love sent to me
Eight maids a-milking,
Seven swans a-swimming,
Six geese a-laying,
Five gold rings,
Four colly birds,
Three French hens,
Two turtle doves
And a partridge in a pear tree.

The ninth day of Christmas
My true love sent to me
Nine drummers drumming,
Eight maids a-milking,
Seven swans a-swimming,
Six geese a-laying,
Five gold rings,
Four colly birds,
Three French hens,
Two turtle doves
And a partridge in a pear tree.

The tenth day of Christmas
My true love sent to me
Ten pipers piping,
Nine drummers drumming,
Eight maids a-milking,
Seven swans a-swimming,
Six geese a-laying,
Five gold rings,
Four colly birds,
Three French hens,
Two turtle doves
And a partridge in a pear tree.

The eleventh day of Christmas
My true love sent to me
Eleven ladies dancing,
Ten pipers piping,
Nine drummers drumming,
Eight maids a-milking,
Seven swans a-swimming,
Six geese a-laying,
Five gold rings,
Four colly birds,
Three French hens,
Two turtle doves.
And a partridge in a pear tree.

The twelfth day of Christmas
My true love sent to me
Twelve lords a-leaping,
Eleven ladies dancing,
Ten pipers piping,
Nine drummers drumming,
Eight maids a-milking,
Seven swans a-swimming,
Six geese a-laying,
Five gold rings,
Four colly birds,
Three French hens,
Two turtle doves
And a partridge in a pear tree.

The Christmas truce

It seems that the spirit of Christmas is sometimes so strong that it can survive in the face of enormous opposition and in the most unlikely places.

This was never more apparent than on Christmas Day 1914.

Britain and Germany were at war. Everyone had hoped that the fighting would be over by Christmas, but instead it was only just getting under way.

The soldiers in the front lines were living in trenches dug out of the earth and conditions were terrible.

A British officer when retelling the events of Christmas Day described it as a beautiful frosty morning with a blue sky.

During the morning the British soldiers realized that their German opponents were coming out of their trenches, and gathering in No-mans Land (an area of land not belonging to either Britain or Germany). The British soldiers were quick to respond and climbed out of their trenches to look.

One of the German soldiers had a camera and photographs were taken and cigarettes exchanged. It must have been an amazing sight; soldiers who the day before had been trying to kill each other and who did not understand each other's language, exchanging cigarettes and taking photographs, only to return to their trenches and resume the fighting when Christmas was over.

It all felt most curious: here were those sausage eating wretches, who had elected to start this infernal European fracas, and in doing so had brought us all into the same muddy pickle as themselves. This was my first sight of them at close quarters. Here they were the actual, practical soldiers of the German army. There was not an atom of hate on either side that day: and yet on our side not for a moment was the will to win the war, and the will to beat them relaxed. It was just like the interval between rounds in a friendly boxing match.

Friday, January 8, 1915.

The Daily Mirror

CERTIFIED CIRCULATION LARGER THAN ANY OTHER DAILY NEWSPAPER IN THE WORLD

WHY D

Pictures and Ne
abroad. You can
Subscription rates
Address—Mar

AN HISTORIC GROUP: BRITISH AND GERMAN SOLDIERS

Christmas flowers

The Christmas Rose

This beautiful creamy white flower originates in mountainous areas, and flowers over the winter between December and March even in the snow.

The flowers were once considered sacred and were used to ward off the plague and all sorts of evil spirits. The roots which are black, give it the name of black hellebore. These roots when dried and powdered cause violent sneezing.

The Poinsettia

This plant, whose leaves turn a beautiful red and look like flowers, comes from Mexico. It was discovered by Dr Poinsett in 1828 and named after him. Its Mexican name translated means 'Flower of the Holy Night'.

There is a legend as to how the plant came to have such lovely red leaves.

One day a little peasant girl was standing by the doors of the church watching enviously as people took in gifts to offer to the statue of the baby Jesus. She was sad that she had nothing to give. An angel appeared to her and said that she should pick some of the plants which grew by the side of the road, and take them as her offering.

The girl picked a large bunch of the green-leaved plants and took them inside. The people in the congregation were very cruel and laughed out loud to see the little girl in her tattered clothes taking a bunch of 'weeds' as an offering. She was very ashamed and her face reddened. As she blushed, the leaves of the plants turned scarlet too and what had looked like ordinary plants appeared to turn into beautiful flowers.

The people were amazed at this miracle and very ashamed that they had laughed.

The scientific explanation of this miracle is in fact that the plant reacts to light — it is photo-periodic. The plants, which start out life as all green, turn red if exposed to 11 hours of light every day for 70 days.

HOW TO MAKE
flower decorations

A Christmas wreath

You will need:

chicken wire
gloves
florist's wire
pliers
greenery such as holly, ivy and yew
moss (you can buy this from florists)
florist's ribbon (ordinary ribbon will go soggy
  outside in the rain).

To make:

Wearing the gloves to protect your hands cut a strip of chicken wire 60 cm long and 15 cm wide.

Bend the wire into a tube shape and twist the cut edges of the wire together with pliers to join it.

Bend the tube into a circle and join the ends.

Wrap the moss round the chicken wire and bind it with florist's wire.

Twist florist's wire around the stems of your holly and yew and then onto the chicken wire until you can't see any wire showing through.

Use florist's wire to attach a bow to the bottom of your wreath, and to fix baubles around it.

The table decoration and the pyramid in the illustrations below are both made by pushing short pieces of greenery, candles, and flowers into something called Oasis, which you can buy from any florist. It is available either in blocks which you can cut into any shape with a kitchen knife, or in pyramids or balls.

Q. What is the difference between illegal and unlawful? A... Unlawful means wrong, and an illegal is a sick bird.
Patient: 'Doctor, my hair is falling out~can you give me something to keep it in?' Doctor: 'Certainly sir~here's a carrier bag.'
Customer to shop assistant~ 'I want a puppy for my little boy.' Assistant: 'I'm sorry sir we don't do exchanges'
Q. Why dont elephants like penguins? A...Because they cant get the paper off with their trunks.
Q. Where would a sick ship go? A...To the 'dock'
John Bendall

The crackers that we buy to pull on Christmas Day are a fairly recent addition to the Christmas tradition. They were invented by a London pastry cook called Tom Smith in the reign of Queen Victoria.

Tom spent a holiday in Paris where he noticed that they sold sugared almonds and various other sweets wrapped in twists of brightly coloured paper. These sweets seemed to be extremely popular, so when he returned home he copied the idea. The new bright wrappings encouraged people to give the sweets to each other as presents, so he began to include love mottoes and riddles inside with the sweets.

The idea of including a 'bang' in the wrapping came later and was the result of Tom gazing into the fire one night and watching the logs crackling. He began to wonder whether it would be possible to make a package which when opened produced a tiny explosion — not too loud, otherwise it would frighten people, but just enough to make them jump. Tom had no idea how to go about making this new type of packaging, but after many experiments he devised the method that is still used today, that of using two pieces of cardboard treated with chemicals which react with a 'crack' when pulled apart.

These early crackers were called 'cosaques', and Tom Smith was keen to make them elegant as well as amusing. He even went so far as to commission quite well-known artists and authors of the day to produce the designs and to write the mottoes. His crackers would have contained gifts such as fans, jewellery, and also head-dresses, in fact all the things that crackers contain today but on a much grander scale.

Tom's idea was so successful that he opened his first factory in 1847 and the business still exists today. In 1983 they produced thirty-six million crackers, enough, if you laid them end to end, to stretch from Norwich, which is where their factory is, to Hong Kong where the novelties are made.

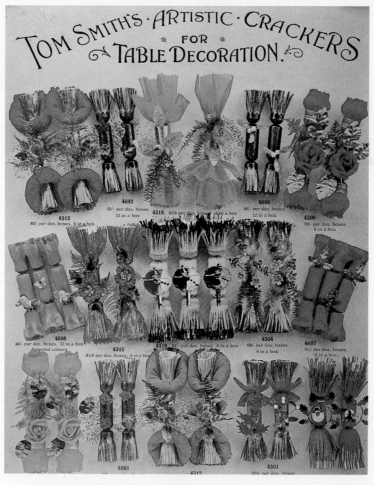

HOW TO MAKE
your own crackers

Making your own Christmas crackers is not difficult, and does mean that you can make each one quite different, and personal.

You will need:

crêpe paper

a cardboard tube for each cracker (the inside of a toilet roll will do plus one extra)

mottoes

hats made from coloured tissue paper

cotton

glue or sticky tape

a small gift. Make sure that whatever you choose will fit into the cardboard tube!

ribbon, tinsel, crêpe paper, and old Christmas cards, to decorate.

To make:

Cut the extra tube in half, and cut one of these pieces in half again.

Take one whole tube and place the two small pieces on either side of it.

Put your hat, gift and motto into the large tube.

Cut a piece of crêpe paper the same length as all three tubes put together, and wide enough to roll round them with about 10 mm overlapping.

Wrap the paper round the tubes and glue or tape into position.

Tie the cotton round the crackers where the tubes meet and pull tight. Do this carefully as the paper can sometimes tear.

Take out the two small tubes, and decorate with glitter, crêpe-paper flowers, or ribbon and write a name on each one.

If you would like to add a crepe paper frill like the one on the crackers shown here, cut two pieces of crepe paper long enough to wrap round the cracker and a quarter of the length. Decorate the edges, and wrap them round the crackers where the long and short tubes meet.

Christmas fun

Christmas has a good effect on adults as far as playing games is concerned. Quite often people who would never normally make fools of themselves can be persuaded to take part in all sorts of nonsense at Christmas.

At one time Christmas was the only time when games were allowed, and people made the most of the holiday for all sorts of sports and relaxation.

The playing of games and fun in general was presided over by a 'Lord of Misrule'. Whoever was appointed had to organize the festivities right up till Candlemas Day.

It might be a good idea to have your own Lord of Misrule this Christmas — someone to decide which games to play, to give prizes to the winners, and make people perform forfeits if they cheat.

Fancy dress parties are always a lot of fun, but people don't always have time to make elaborate costumes at Christmas time. If you would like a theme to your party which does not involve too much dressing up, try having a hat party, or a mask party. You can make a hat or a mask for each of your guests or you could ask them to bring their own and give a prize to the most original.

A simple hat shape can be made by cutting a circle of thin card about the size of a small plate (bigger if you want your hat to be very tall or very wide) and cutting a section out of it, as shown. The bigger the piece that you cut out, the taller and thinner your hat will be. Glue or tape the two edges together, and decorate with painted or cut-out shapes. To make sure that your hat stays on, make two holes — one on either side of it — and thread very thin elastic through, knotting it on each side. Make sure that you allow the right amount of elastic for each hat.

Masks are also easy to make and are fun because people don't recognise each other straight away. Cut out a shape which will fit over the nose and which has holes cut out for the eyes. Make newspaper templates until you have got the shape

right, then draw around it onto thin card. Make a hole on each side of the mask and thread elastic through to fit the head.

You could try some of these:

Cat — use black card and add white pipe cleaner whiskers.

Bird — stick a beak over the nose section and stick on 'feathers' cut from crêpe paper.

Witch — make a 'nose' from papier maché complete with warts, and a witches hat to complete the outfit.

Queen — use gold card, and old beads and sequins for jewels.

When people arrive at your party, it is a good idea to play a game which helps them to get to know all the other people there.

Partners

Before your guests arrive write the names of two halves of a partnership on separate pieces of paper. Here are some examples, but there are all sorts of couples that you could use:

Bonnie and Clyde
Laurel and Hardy
Sooty and Sweep
Bacon and egg
Knife and fork

When people arrive, attach one of the pieces of paper to their back with a safety pin. Don't tell them who they are. Each person must then ask questions to find out their identity. The answer to each question can only be Yes or No.

For example: Am I a person?
Am I historical?
Am I alive?
Am I a glove puppet?

Until they discover who they are and find their partner.

Flip the kipper

Before the party cut fish shapes from newspaper and decorate them. Divide your guests into either teams (if there are a lot), or couples. Give each team or pair a rolled up newspaper.

The object of the game is to hit the floor behind each 'kipper' with the newspaper so that it travels along the ground. The first person or team to get to the other end of the room is the winner.

If you are going to play games at your party, it is nice to have prizes to give to the winners. These do not have to be very much. Perhaps you could make

some of the edible presents described earlier in the book, or buy a large bag of mixed sweets.

Demon Patience

This is a good game for waking up the family after a large Christmas lunch. I would not advise you to play it too soon afterwards, though, as it can get quite hectic.

Someone in the family is sure to know how to play patience! This is a version which livens the ordinary game up quite a bit.

To play you will need a pack of cards per person, and floor space.

Each person starts to play by setting out the cards. The difference is that instead of only being able to use your own cards you can also take any upturned card showing in the other person's game to complete your own. Once the cards are laid out, get someone to shout Go, and let the race begin.

A memory game

This game is far less boisterous and quite difficult.

You will need:

A tray
a piece of paper and a pen per person
a cloth to cover the tray
about 20 small objects.

Allow the players to look at the objects for 1 minute. Cover the tray and give everyone 5 minutes to remember as many objects as they can.

The Yes No game

Sit in a circle. Each player asks the person on his or her right a question. Keep it very simple. The words Yes and No are banned. If anyone uses them they are out of the game. The winner is the last person not to have used these words. If people are getting too good, speed the game up.

CHIMNEYS & REINDEER

37 ☆

38 LAND ON TOP OF FLATS. LIFT OUT OF ORDER. BACK TO SQUARE 14.

39 ☆

40

41

42 ALL DONE TILL NEXT YEAR.

36 HITCH A RIDE ON AN AEROPLANE, GO ON TO SQUARE 40.

35

34 NEARLY DAWN, SPEED ON TO 41.

33

32 CHIMNEY NEEDS SWEEPING. STOP FOR CLEAN-UP. LOSE 1 TURN.

31

25 SLEIGH BRAKES FAIL, CRASH LAND ON SQUARE 22 AND LOSE 1 TURN FOR REPAIRS.

26

27

28 CHILDREN AWAKE. LOSE 1 TURN WHILE YOU WAIT FOR THEM TO GO TO SLEEP.

29

30 NO CHIMNEY. CENTRAL HEATING. LOSE 1 TURN LOOKING FOR ANOTHER WAY IN.

24 ALL STOP FOR WELL EARNED REST, LOSE 1 GO.

23

CRASH!

22

21

20 PARCELS NOT LABELLED LOSE 1 TURN.

19 BEAUTIFUL CLEAR SKY GO ON TO SQUARE 29.

13

14

15 LOST PARCEL. GO BACK TO 8.

16

17 FATHER CHRISTMAS STUCK IN CHIMNEY. LOSE 1 TURN.

18 ☆

12

11 RIDE A SHOOTING STAR, GO ON TO 21.

10

9

8

7

1 BAD WEATHER OVER NORTH POLE, THROW A 6 TO START.

WEST EAST

2

3 FLYING FAST TO MAKE UP FOR LOST TIME. GO ON TO SQUARE 8.

4

5

6

78

Good King Wenceslas

Good King Wenceslas look'd out,
On the Feast of Stephen,
When the snow lay round about,
Deep and crisp and even;
Brightly shone the moon that night,
Though the frost was cruel,
When a poor man came in sight,
Gath'ring winter fuel.

'Hither page, and stand by me,
If thou know'st it, telling.
Yonder peasant, who is he?
Where and what his dwelling?'
'Sire, he lives a good league hence,
Underneath the mountain,
Right against the forest fence,
By Saint Agnes' fountain.'

A Christmas 'box'

Christmas is a time when people have always tried to think of others and give money generously to the poor. Churches had 'Alms Boxes' where people could put their gifts on Christmas Day. The day after Christmas was the day when these boxes were broken open, and the contents distributed to the poor, and because of this it became known as Boxing Day.

There is evidence that this custom dates back as far as Roman times, and continued up to the time of the Puritans when all such Christmas customs were banned. Indeed the churches were closed, so the alms boxes had no chance to be filled.

The tradition of giving out 'Christmas Boxes' is all that remains of the custom.

Christmas Boxes were sums of money handed out the day after Christmas to those people who had provided a good service during the year: for example, the postman, milkman, and refuse collectors.

This tradition still continues today although it usually happens before Christmas now, as these people don't call on Boxing Day.

The two St Stephens

The 26 December is also the Feast of St Stephen, the first Christian martyr to be killed for his faith. He lived at about the same time as Jesus, and was stoned to death.

It was on this day that we are told in the song . . . 'Good King Wenceslas looked out on the Feast of Stephen . . .'

One of the legends about St Stephen is that he worked in Herod's kitchen.

Stephen out of the kitchen came, with a boar's head in hand:
He saw a star was fair and bright over Bethlehem stand:
He cast down the boar's head and went into the hall:
'I forsake thee, King Herod, and thy works all;
There is a child in Bethlehem born is better than us all.'

(carol written in 1400)

There was another St Stephen who was a Swedish missionary. Although his feast day was some way away from Christmas, somehow the two celebrations have become mixed up.

The second St Stephen is said to have loved horses, and many customs were practised on his feast day connected with them.

In Munich, men on horseback would ride round the inside of the churches, their mounts gaily decorated with ribbons.

In some other countries including the British Isles, horses were 'bled'. This meant letting a small amount of blood, not enough to harm the horse, to get rid of evil spirits that might cause illness during the following year.

The traditional Boxing Day hunt may well be a modern tradition stemming from the feast of this St Stephen.

The snowflake

Before I melt
Come, look at me!
This lovely, icy filigree!
Of a great forest
In one night
I make a wilderness
Of white:
By skyey cold
Of crystals made,
All softly on
Your fingers laid,
I pause, that you
My beauty see:
Breathe, and I vanish
Instantly.

Walter de la Mare

Herod asked his priests and scribes where Christ was to be born.

Can you tell me where Christ will be born? I have gifts for him and would like to worship him.

It is prophesy that he will be born in Bethlehem your Majesty

...and he in turn told the wise men.

The child that you seek is in Bethlehem. When you find him send word to me as I have gifts for him too.

When they arrived in Bethlehem...

...the star guided them to Mary and Joseph's house.

Joseph was amazed to find the wise men at his door in the middle of the night!

The Kings worshipped the baby and offered their gifts

Meanwhile at Herod's palace....

83

Continued on page 98

He's behind you

'He's behind you' — this is the cry that we all associate with pantomime.

Pantomime is an entertainment for all the family. Sometimes it might get a bit risqué, but it is not offensive and is based around a formula which doesn't change. There is always a villain to boo and hiss, a principal boy who's played by a girl, and a dame who's played by a man. Music, songs, comedy, acrobatics, transformations, and finally the triumph of good over evil all go to make up the traditional pantomime.

The earliest forms of pantomime probably go right back to the 'Feast of Fools', and the masques presided over by the Lord of Misrule. In both of these a topsy-turvy world was created where all was not as it seemed; men dressed as women, slaves were masters, and chaos was normal.

The pantomime contains all these things, but to find a more recent ancestor we have to go to sixteenth-century Italy, to the Commedia dell'Arte. This was a tradition of unscripted plays performed by travelling players. They were based around the characters of Columbine and Harlequin (the lovers), Pantaloon (the villain), and a clown. These comedy plays were very popular and were performed all over Italy. Eventually their success took them to

Paris and then on to London. In England they were called the Harlequinade and were performed as a comic interlude in a full-length play. The word pantomime means 'all in mime', and these original 'mini plays' were mimed.

John Rich at the Lincoln's Inn Field Theatre in 1717 staged the first complete Harlequinade, which was a combination of a classical play and the Commedia dell'Arte characters.

It was John Rich who also introduced the transformations into the performance. These began as quite simple effects such as using trap-doors to make people disappear, but as time went on they became more and more complicated and more imaginative.

It was in Victorian times that the link between pantomime and Christmas grew. Before this they had been performed at any time of the year. Gradually the original characters died out and fairy tales took over as the themes.

When the music hall was popular, artists would use the pantomimes to promote their acts. They would change the plots sometimes so that they were unrecognizable to fit in their latest songs and sketches. Today the pantomime is still very popular although many people criticize its predictable formula.

HOW TO WRITE
coded thank you letters

After Christmas it is a good idea to write to all the people who gave you presents to say thank you (otherwise they might think that you didn't like them and not send you any more).

To make your letters more fun to write and to receive, you could write them in code as shown below.

It is a good idea to write the proper letter very small, upside down at the bottom of the page so that if people can't work out the code they can cheat. If you don't do this, people might never know what it was all about, and you will have wasted a stamp.

86

The Old Year

The Old Year's gone away
    To nothingness and night:
We cannot find him all the day
    Nor hear him in the night:
He left no footstep, mark or place
    In either shade or sun:
The last year he'd a neighbour's face,
    In this he's known by none.

All nothing everywhere:
    Mists we on mornings see
Have more of substance when they're here
    And more of form than he.
He was a friend by every fire,
    In every cot and hall —
A guest to every heart's desire,
    And now he's nought at all.

Old papers thrown away,
    Old garments cast aside,
The talk of yesterday
    All things identified;
But times once torn away
    No voices can recall:
The eve of New Year's Day
    Left the Old Year lost to all.

John Clare

New Year

New Year's Eve has always been seen as a perfect opportunity to look back over the year that is about to end, make resolutions for the year to come, and try to ensure as much good luck for it as possible.

Many of the customs that exist are based around making a fresh start. It is traditional to return anything borrowed and clean the house from top to bottom.

The expression 'ring out the old year and ring in the new', came about because all over the country the church bells were rung to signal the end of the year.

The departing year was let out of the houses by opening the windows and doors before midnight, and shutting them as twelve o'clock struck. Sometimes the evil spirits that might have been lurking in dark corners were driven away by banging trays and ringing bells.

Once the doors and windows were shut, the luck for the next year would be determined by the first person to enter the house.

First footing

The first person to enter the house on New Year's Eve has to be a complete stranger if you are to have good luck for the following year. He must also have dark hair (or red in some places) and be carrying a piece of coal, a spray of evergreen, a pinch of salt and a slice of bread. These things are to symbolize warmth, hospitality, and long life.

Your first-footer would bring bad luck if it was a woman, or someone cross-eyed or flat-footed.

The first-footer should enter the house by the front door and leave by the back door, to take good luck right through the house.

If you were unfortunate enough to be visited by someone not fitting the right description, then you could cancel the bad luck by throwing salt on the fire.

Hogmanay

Since the days when the Puritans banned the celebration of Christmas, the people of Scotland have celebrated New Year's Eve almost as much as Christmas. In fact many of the traditions associated with Christmas were moved to New Year and stayed there.

In Scotland the celebration is called Hogmanay.

The word is thought to have originally come from the Ancient Greek word 'Hagmena' which meant Holy moon, and was used to describe the Druid ceremony of cutting the sacred mistletoe.

The word 'Hogmanay' is now used for the New Year celebrations in Scotland.

Hogmanay, and indeed New Year's Eve in England, would not be complete without the singing of 'Auld Lang Syne'. These words written by the poet Robert Burns are traditionally sung at midnight in the company of friends and family.

Should auld acquaintance be forgot,
 And never brought to mind,
Should auld acquaintance be forgot,
 And days of Lang Syne.
For Auld Lang Syne, my dear,
 For Auld Lang Syne,
We'll tak'a cup o' kindness yet,
 For Auld Lang Syne.

In Stonehaven in Scotland a custom exists called 'swinging the fireballs'. This is thought to have been originated by the fishermen of the district, although no one knows quite what its purpose was.

The 'fireballs' are wire baskets filled with wood and cones. These are set fire to and swung around the head by long handles.

In nearby Cumrie a similar procession takes place using long poles, the tops of which are bound in sacking and set fire to.

Both these dramatic and rather mysterious processions are accompanied by the traditional pipe band.

The old and new years are sometimes represented by an old man (Old Father Time) and a young child.

In the Channel Isles a figure of Old Father Time is buried in the sand to signify the end of the old year's reign.

In Paris the new year is welcomed in by the hooting of car horns, and the sounding of ships' sirens is a familiar sign of the new year in harbours all round the world.

Wassailing

The word wassail comes from the Anglo-Saxon words 'was hael' which meant good health.

The custom of wassailing involved groups of people walking around the villages on New Year's Eve with a wassail bowl, made of applewood. This bowl was filled with a drink called 'lambswool', which was hot ale, spices, sugar, and eggs, with roast apples floating on the top. People paid a small amount of money to drink from the bowl, as it was considered to be lucky to do so. They then refilled the bowl.

Fruit tree wassailing took place not only at new year but at other times such as Halloween. It involved the firing of guns into the fruit trees to drive away the evil spirits and ensure a good crop for the year.

The Chinese New Year

The Gregorian calendar, which is the one that we use, is not used all over the world. Many countries have a different method of calculating the year and start their year at a different time.

The Chinese calendar is calculated by the sun and the moon. To keep this system accurate a month is added every so often.

The Chinese New Year begins somewhere between 21 January and 19 February and is calculated by the appearance of the new moon.

Every year is named after a different animal and the people born within that year are supposed to have certain characteristics associated with it.

You can work out which animal sign you were born under by the chart below.

Rat	1972
Ox	1973
Tiger	1974
Rabbit	1975

Dragon	1976	Monkey	1980
Snake	1977	Cockerel	1981
Horse	1978	Dog	1982
Ram	1979	Pig	1983

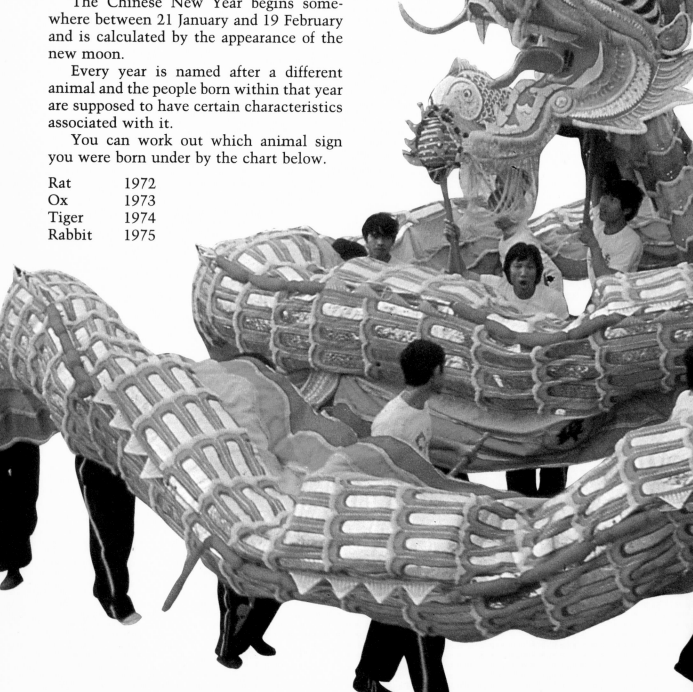

The Chinese New Year is called 'Yuan Tan' and is celebrated not only in China but in Chinese communities all over the world.

New Year's Day is considered to be everybody's birthday and even those born a few days before it are one year old on this day.

The Chinese believe that evil spirits are common at this time, and some of their customs are based around driving them away. Firecrackers are set off in the hope that the noise will drive them away, and doors and windows are sealed up to prevent them getting into the house while the family sit down to their New Year meal.

The most spectacular part of the celebrations are the street parades which are colourful and noisy affairs. These have as their centre-piece the symbol of good luck, the dragon.

The parades are lit by thousands of lanterns.

The dragon itself is made from cloth or paper on a bamboo frame and its bulging eyes and roaring mouth are worked by people underneath.

These dragons can be very large, sometimes needing as many as fifty people to support them and make them writhe and twist along the streets.

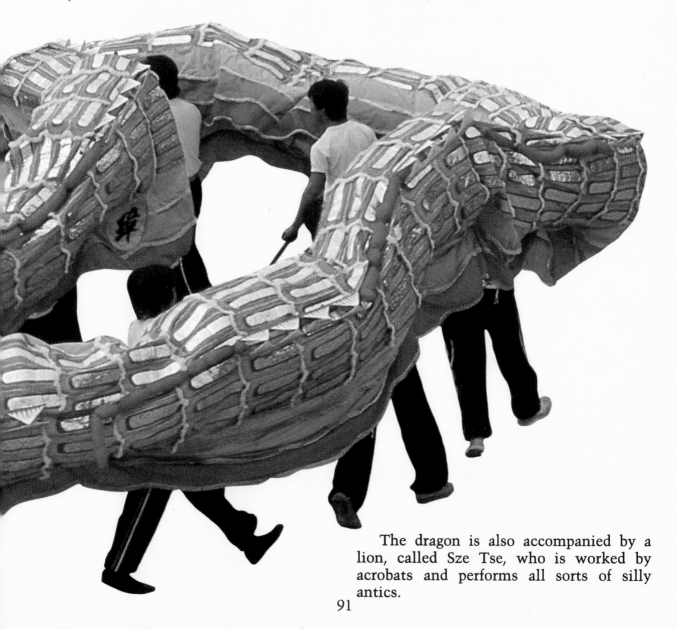

The dragon is also accompanied by a lion, called Sze Tse, who is worked by acrobats and performs all sorts of silly antics.

The budgie's New Year message

Get a little tin of bird-seed,
Pour it in my little trough.
If you don't, you little twit, I'll
Bite your little finger off.

Kit Wright

New Year in other lands

Holi is the Hindu New Year which because of the way the Hindu calendar is calculated falls in February or early March. It is celebrated by the lighting of bonfires onto which are thrown coconuts and grains of barley as a sacrifice to the fire, the rest of the food being eaten afterwards as part of a feast. Images of the Demon Holika are burned to signify the triumph of good over evil.

Divali is also a new year celebration but of a more commercial kind when business-men draw up contracts for the following year, settle accounts, and pray for a year of prosperity.

The Jewish New Year, called Rosh Hashannah, is in September or October. It is celebrated by a special meal of sweet foods to symbolize a happy new year, and by visiting synagogues to pray and to celebrate the creation of the earth.

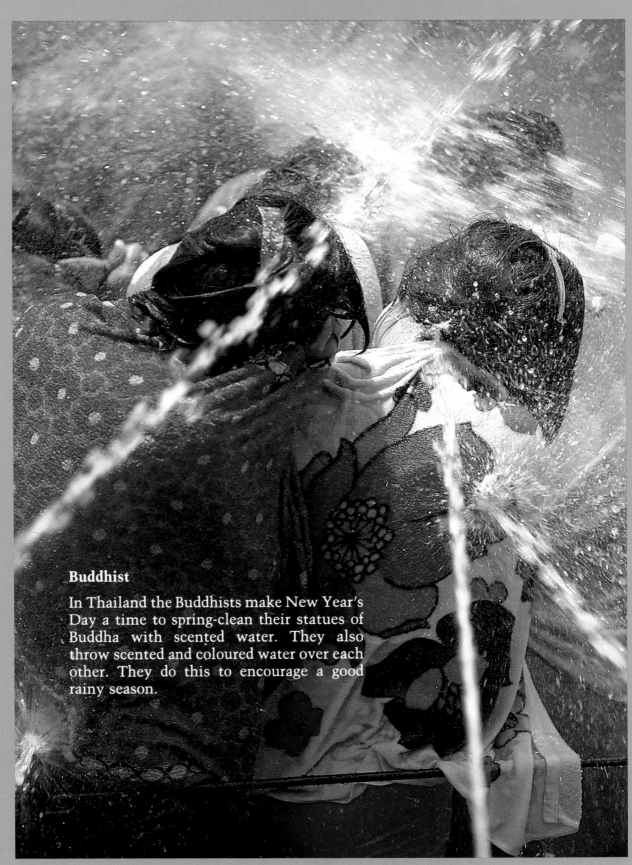

Buddhist

In Thailand the Buddhists make New Year's Day a time to spring-clean their statues of Buddha with scented water. They also throw scented and coloured water over each other. They do this to encourage a good rainy season.

EPIPHANY

Twelfth Night song

See them! There they go,
Three great kings go riding through snow,
Three kings on three horses
Go riding on their way
To see Him, Jesu, born a king today.

Drums beat as they come,
Joyfully riding to see Mary's son,
The new-born King.
To Bethlehem they come to see Him,
Jesu, Mary's new-born son.

Furs they brought the Child,
Furs warm and soft, from forest wild,
And gay songs to sing,
To Him they did bring, to Him, to Jesu,
Tiny little sweet boy Child.

Epiphany and Candlemas

Epiphany

Twelfth Night, or Epiphany as it is known in the Church, is on 6 January. The word Epiphany means 'showing', in this case when the baby Jesus was shown to the three wise men for them to spread the news of his birth. The Church celebrates the arrival in Bethlehem of the wise men to worship and offer their gifts.

A member of the Royal household still presents gifts of gold, frankincense, and myrrh at the Chapel Royal in remembrance of the event.

When Twelfth Night marked the end of the holiday it used to be celebrated almost as much as Christmas Day itself. Now it is rather a sad day when all the decorations are packed away, and the house returns to normal.

In many other countries it is still an important festival. Often it is a day associated with children, who are given presents in memory of the gifts brought by the wise men.

In Spain and France the children go out in search of the wise men, and take gifts of hay for the camels.

In Germany it is traditional for the boys of the villages to carry a star round the streets as a symbol of the star which guided the Three Kings.

A Twelfth Night tradition which has died out completely in England, but is still practised in many European countries, is the baking of a Twelfth Night cake and the appointment of a king and queen for the day.

The Twelfth Night cake had a bean and a pea baked inside it. Whoever found the bean was the king, and the person who found the pea was the queen. They ruled for just one day.

If a man found the pea, then he gave it to the girl that he would like to be his queen.

In the seventeenth century this custom was very elaborate, and not only involved appointing a king and queen, but all the courtiers as well.

The cakes were very beautiful, and so as not to spoil them, the court was chosen by pulling names out of a hat.

Candlemas

Candlemas is on 2 February. This was traditionally the end of Christmas, and used to be the day that the decorations were taken down.

The superstition was that for every decoration left up after this date, you would see a goblin.

We don't know for sure why Twelfth Night took over as the time to dismantle all the decorations. Perhaps keeping up the festivities for such a long time became impractical. However it did take over and people still respect the tradition of removing the tree and all the trimmings on that date. It is still considered to be bad luck to leave any decorations up afterwards, although we no longer believe the goblin theory.

Down with rosemary, and so
Down with bays and mistletoe;
Down with holly, ivy, all
Wherewith ye dressed the Christmas hall;
That so the superstitious find
No one least branch there left behind;
For look, how many leaves there be
Neglected there, maids, trust in me,
So many goblins you shall see.

The wise men and the star

The three kings who were guided by a star to Bethlehem were not kings of countries, but were probably high officials of some kind, or astrologers.

We believe that there were three, although the Bible does not give a number.

It is thought that they were: Melchior who brought gold, Caspar who brought frankincense, and Balthazar who brought myrrh.

What star they followed still remains a mystery. If we have dated Christ's birth correctly, then it cannot be any of the comets that we know of. There was some feeling that it might have been Halley's comet, which appears to us every 76 years, and would have been very bright in the east. This would not have been possible, though, as the nearest date for the comet to have been seen was 12 years before Christ's birth.

People at the time were very aware of the stars and believed that important events were forecast in the night sky.

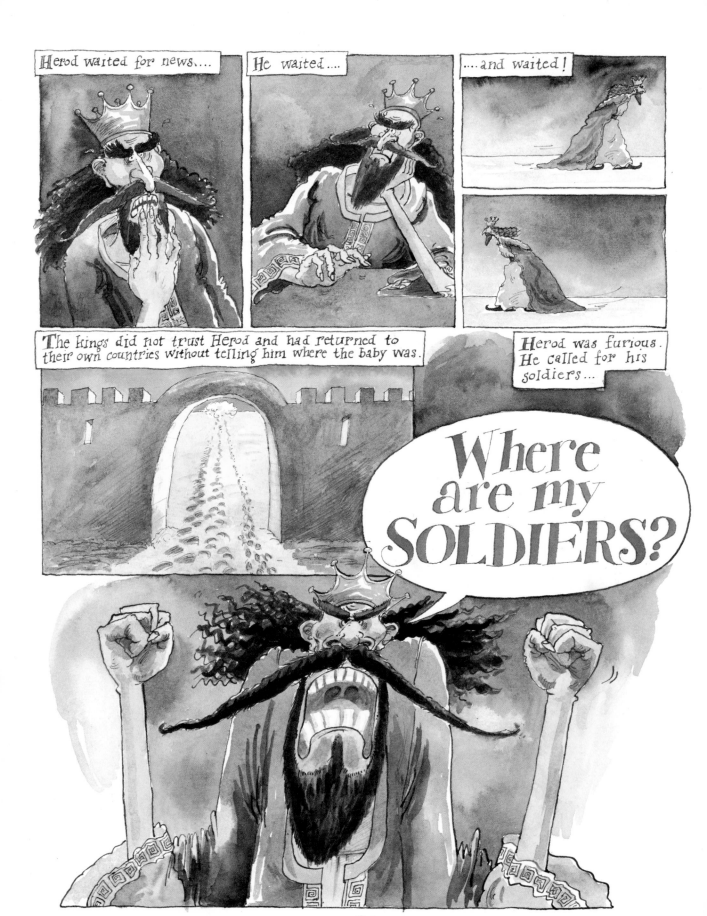

...and gave them terrible orders

Those Wise men tricked me but I will show them

I want every boy child under two years old in Bethlehem KILLED

But Joseph had a dream....

BETHLEHEM EGYPT

And when the soldiers came looking for baby Jesus...

Mary and Joseph were safely on their way...

... to Egypt, where they stayed until they heard of Herod's death, and it was safe to return.

~The Daily Tablet~ HEROD DEAD

Not the end...the beginning

99

Christmas around the world

Christmas is celebrated all over the world. In every country the customs and traditions vary slightly, but one thing which is the same everywhere is the spirit of joy and friendship, when people take the time to think of other people.

America

America is such a large country that there are a variety of different customs and traditions within it. Many of the decorations and celebrations are the same as in Britain, and other communities who have settled in America have taken their own festivals with them.

The American people took the idea of Father Christmas very much to heart. It was they who shaped him into the red-coated, white-bearded, jolly old gentleman that we know today. He also has two homes in America.

In Torrington, Connecticut, there is a Christmas village where Santa and his elves give out presents. In Wilmington, New York, on the side of Whiteface Mountain, a man called Arto Monaco designed a permanent home for Santa Claus. It has a blacksmith (for the reindeer), a chapel, and a post office. Every year over 100,000 people visit this village.

There is a town in America called Santa Claus. All the letters which are posted in America addressed to him go there to be dealt with (over three million every Christmas time). There is also a park with a coloured statue of him 23 feet high.

In 1924, a national living Christmas tree was planted in Washington D.C. Every year the President of the USA ceremonially turns on the lights.

Italy

The Italian people treat the day before Christmas as a fast day, and eat and drink very little.

The centre-piece of the decorations in the houses and the churches is the crib. They are called 'il presepe', and are sometimes very beautiful and elaborate.

The time for exchanging gifts in Italy is 6 January, which is when the wise men gave their gifts to Jesus. These gifts are delivered by 'la Befana', a white witch who flies down the chimney with them on her broomstick.

La Befana is supposed to have been one of the people who denied Mary and Joseph hospitality when they arrived in Bethlehem. She has been leaving gifts at every house since then, to make up for her error. The gifts are left in the children's shoes, which they place before the fire in readiness.

Germany

Many of the British Christmas customs originated in Germany, and are familiar to us. There are some differences, though. For example, St Nicholas is considered only to be the messenger who takes the Christmas requests up to heaven. The person who delivers them is the messenger of the Christchild and is called Christkind, or Christkindl.

St Nicholas also takes with him to Heaven a report on each child to make sure that they have been good. If they have not, a bundle of rods is left on the doorstep to beat them with.

Spain

In Spain the festivities centre less on the home, and are more carnival-like street celebrations. On Christmas Eve people go out and sing and dance, sometimes right through till the early hours of Christmas morning. Those who are going to mass do so at midnight, and then go back to their houses for a family meal.

The children get their presents on 6 January. They are brought by the wise men, and so, as well as leaving out their shoes to be filled with presents, they also leave straw for the camels.

The Spanish celebrations last right up till Epiphany.

Holland

The Dutch celebrate St Nicholas Day on 6 December with parties.

St Nicholas arrives in person on the last Saturday in November, accompanied by Black Peter.

Thousands of children and adults gather to watch him arrive as he travels on his white horse.

It was the Dutch settlers in America who inadvertently gave Santa Claus his name. Their word for him was Sinter Klaass and when people said it incorrectly it became Santa Claus.

The Dutch also carry on the tradition of the Twelfth Night cake with a bean baked in it. The person who finds the bean gets special treatment during the day and can choose their favourite meals and make people do things for them.

France

Christmas Day is celebrated in France as it is in England by all the family coming together.

The children leave their shoes in front of the fire on Christmas Eve, and Père Noël (Father Christmas) leaves gifts in them overnight.

The midnight service on Christmas Eve is traditionally followed by a meal called 'le reveillon'.

In northern France children are given their gifts on 6 December, which is St Nicholas day, instead of on Christmas Day.

Australia

Christmas in Australia falls during mid-summer when the weather is at its hottest, and people are taking their summer holidays.

Many of the differences in customs and traditions between England and Australia are due to the dramatic difference in temperature, for example it is not surprising that Yule logs are not lit and hot punches are not drunk.

The fact that the weather is so hot means that much of the celebration of Christmas goes on outside. Christmas lunch is often eaten on the beach, complete with Christmas tree, and crackers, although the turkey is eaten cold with salads, rather than hot as we eat it in England.

One spectacular outdoor event is the singing of carols in the city parks on Christmas Eve. Hundreds of thousands of people take part in the singing, and the whole thing is illuminated by candle-light.

It is Father Christmas who brings the presents to Australian children on Christmas Eve. These are usually opened at breakfast time on Christmas Day. Father Christmas must be very hot in his woolly robes and thick white beard!

Two popular flowers used to decorate houses are Christmas bush and Christmas bell. Christmas bush is a mass of tiny flowers growing in clumps, and Christmas bell, as its name suggests, is a bell-shaped flower with yellow edges.

Boxing Day centres around the children, and often involves a trip to one of Australia's many entertainment complexes.

Christmas in two lands

There it is cold, or there is snow —
And holly, fires and mistletoe,
And carols sung out in the street
By children, walking through the sleet.
Church bells break the frozen air
Ringing loudly everywhere.
There is where white winter glory
Comes to tell the Christmas story.

Here it is hot, the sun is gold —
And turns tired when day is old,
Christmas carols are sung at night
Somewhere outside, by candle-light.
Church bells ring out in the heat
And call to people in the street.
The Christmas story here is told
In summer, when the sun is gold.

Joan Mellings

Mexico

The Mexican people begin their celebrations on 16 December by remembering the journey that Mary and Joseph made to Bethlehem.

This part of the celebration is called 'las Posadas', which means resting place, and takes the form of a procession of people who act out the turning away of Mary and Joseph from the inns in Bethlehem.

The procession is divided into pilgrims and innkeepers, all carrying candles. As they reach each house the pilgrims ask for shelter. The innkeepers turn them away, telling them that there is no room.

Eventually the innkeepers relent and the procession enters the house where the people pray at a home-made crib, which stands on an altar.

Las Posadas takes place every evening from 16 December to Christmas Eve, and after each one there is a party.

A centre-piece for the children at these parties is the 'piñata'. This is a decorated container, which can be any shape (birds, aeroplanes and dolls are popular), suspended outside above the garden.

The children are blindfolded and given a long stick. They then try one by one to break open the piñata which is filled with sweets and fruits. Eventually someone manages to burst it and there is a scramble for all the goodies.

Sometimes there is a shock when the piñata has been filled with water instead of sweets, and everyone gets very wet.

The Mexican people do most of their celebrating before Christmas Day itself, which is usually a quiet family day.

The day for exchanging presents in Mexico is 6 January which is Epiphany.

Israel

It is to Bethlehem in particular that we look over Christmas time, as the birthplace of Christ. But how do they celebrate it there now?

Christmas in Bethlehem attracts thousands of pilgrims of a variety of religions to the church built on the spot where it is believed that Jesus was born. The Church of the Nativity has a silver star to mark the place, and above it fifteen silver lamps always burn. Around the star is the inscription 'Here of the Virgin Mary Jesus Christ was born'.

On Christmas Eve a service is sung in Latin, at the end of which a model of the Baby Jesus is laid in a manger by the star.

After the service many pilgrims then go out to the fields around Bethlehem to sit where the shepherds heard the news. These fields have changed very little; shepherds still graze their flocks there today.

The Stones of Plouhinec

In parts of Brittany are found groups of the great stones known as menhirs, arranged in circles or avenues, like tall, rough-hewn pillars. Country people will tell you that long ago they were set up by the kerions, the fairy dwarfs, and that beneath them the kerions hid their gold and treasure. Each group of stones has its own legend, and this is the story of the Stones of Plouhinec.

Near Plouhinec, there lies a barren stretch of moor where only coarse grass grows, and the yellow broom of Brittany. On this plain stand the stones of Plouhinec, two long rows of them.

On the edge of the moor lived a farmer with his sister Rozennik. Rozennik was young and pretty, and she had many suitors, yet she saved her smiles for Bernez, a poor lad who worked on her brother's farm; but the farmer refused to consider Bernez as a suitor until he could show him his pockets full of gold.

One Christmas Eve, while the farmer was feasting his men, there came a knock on the door, and outside in the cold wind stood an old beggar who asked for shelter for the night. He looked a sly, artful old rogue, but because it was Christmas Eve, he was made welcome and given a place by the fire. After supper the farmer took him out to the stable and said that he might sleep there, on a pile of straw. In the stable were the ox who drew the farmer's plough and the donkey who carried to market whatever the farmer had to sell.

The beggar was just falling asleep when midnight struck, and, as everyone knows, at midnight on Christmas Eve all the beasts in a stable can speak to each other, in memory of that first Christmas in the stable at Bethlehem.

'It is a cold night,' said the donkey.

As soon as the beggar heard the donkey speak, he pretended to be asleep and snoring, but he kept very wide awake.

'No colder,' replied the ox, 'than it will be on New Year's Eve when the stones of Plouhinec go down to the river to drink and leave their treasure uncovered. Only once in every hundred years that comes to pass.' The ox looked at the beggar, snoring on the straw. 'If this old man knew what we know, he would be off, seven nights from now, to fill his pockets from the kerions' hoard.'

'Small good would it do him,' said the donkey, 'unless he carried a bunch of crows-

foot and a five-leaved trefoil. Without those plants, the stones would crush him when they returned.'

'Even the crowsfoot and the five-leaved trefoil would not be enough,' said the ox, 'for whoever takes the treasure must offer in exchange a Christian soul or the stolen treasure will turn to dust. And though a man may easily find crowsfoot, and he may, if he searches long enough, find a five-leaved trefoil, where will he find a Christian man willing to die for him?'

'That is true enough,' agreed the donkey; and the two beasts went on to talk of other matters.

But the beggar had heard enough. He was away from the farm at first light, and for six days he searched the countryside for crowsfoot and trefoil. He found the crowsfoot soon enough, and he found trefoil, but none with more than three leaves; until on the last day of the old year, he found a five-leaved trefoil. Eagerly he hurried back to the moor.

But he found someone there before him. Young Bernez had brought his midday meal to eat beneath the largest of the stones, and he was spending the few spare minutes that remained before he had to return to work carving a cross upon the stone.

'What are you doing?' asked the old beggar, who recognized him as one of the men from the farmhouse where he had spent Christmas Eve.

Bernez smiled, 'This holy sign may be of help to someone one day. It is as good a way as any of passing an idle moment, to carve a cross on a stone.'

'That is so,' replied the beggar; but while he was speaking he was remembering the look in Bernez' eyes as he watched Rozennik at the feasting on Christmas Eve, and a cunning thought came into his head. 'What would you do,' he asked, 'if you had your pockets full of gold?'

'Why,' said Bernez, 'I would go to the farmer and ask for Rozennik for my wife. He would not refuse me then.'

The beggar leant his head close to Bernez. 'I can tell you how to fill your pockets with gold, and a sack or two besides.'

And he told Bernez what he had learnt from the ox and the ass; all save how a bunch of crowsfoot and a five-leaved trefoil were necessary if one was not to be crushed by the stones, and how a Christian soul must be offered in exchange for the gold. When he had finished, Bernez' eyes shone and he clasped the old man's hand.

'You are a good friend indeed, to share your good fortune with me. I will meet you here before midnight.' He finished carving his cross and ran back to work; whilst the beggar chuckled to himself at how easily he had found someone to die in exchange for the gold.

Before midnight they were waiting together, Bernez and the beggar, hidden behind a clump of broom in the darkness. No sooner had midnight struck than there was a noise as of a great thundering, the ground shook, and the huge stones heaved themselves out of the earth and began to move down to the river. 'Now!' cried the beggar. They ran and looked into the pits where the stones had stood, and there, at the bottom of each pit, was a heap of treasure. The beggar opened the sacks he had brought with him and began to fill them hastily; but Bernez, his heart full of the thought of Rozennik, filled only his pockets with the gold.

It seemed no more than a moment later that the earth began to tremble again and the ground echoed as though to the tramp of a giant army marching. The stones, having drunk from the river, were returning to their places. Bernez cried out in horror as he saw them loom out of the darkness. 'Quickly, quickly, or we shall be crushed to death!' But the old beggar laughed and held up his bunch of crowsfoot and his five-leaved trefoil. 'Not I,' he said, 'for I have these to protect me. But you are lost, and it is as well for me, since unless a Christian soul is given in exchange, my treasure will crumble away in the morning.'

With terror, Bernez saw that he had spoken the truth, for the first of the stones moved aside when it reached the beggar, and after it the other stones passed on either side of him, leaving him untouched as they came near to Bernez.

The young man was too afraid to try to escape. He covered his face when he saw the largest stone of all bear down on him. But above the very spot where Bernez crouched, trembling, the stone paused, towering over him as though to protect him, while all the other stones had to move aside and pass him by. And when Bernez dared to look up, he saw that the stone which sheltered him was the stone upon which he had carved a cross.

Not until all the other stones were in their places did it move on to where its own pit showed dark, with the shining treasure at the bottom. On its way it overtook the beggar, stumbling along with his heavy sacks of gold. He heard it come after him and held out the bunch of crowsfoot and the five-leaved trefoil. But because of the cross carved upon it, the magic herbs had no longer any power over the stone, and it went blindly on, crushing the old beggar beneath it. And it passed on to its own place and settled into the earth again until another hundred years should have gone by. Bernez ran back to the farm as fast as his legs could carry him; and when, in the morning, he showed his pockets full of gold, the farmer did not refuse to give him his sister. And as for Rozennik, she did not say no, for she would have had him anyway, had the choice rested with her.

The fir tree

Out in the forest stood a pretty little fir-tree. It grew in a good place where the sun could get to it, and there was plenty of air and the companionship of many larger trees round about, both fir and pine. But the little fir-tree's one thought was to grow. It took no notice of the warm sunshine and the fresh air. It paid no attention to the country children who went by chattering when they were out gathering strawberries or raspberries. They would often pass that way with a whole crock full, or with strawberries threaded on straws, and then they would sit down by the little tree and say, 'Oh, what a pretty little baby tree it is!' But that wasn't at all the kind of thing the tree wanted to hear.

The year after, it was taller by a long new shoot, and the year after that by an even longer one, for you can always tell how many years a fir-tree has been growing by the number of spaces it has between its rings of branches.

'Oh, if only I were a big tree like the others!' sighed the little tree. 'Then I could spread my branches far out all round me and see the wide world from my top. The birds would build their nests among my branches, and when the wind blew I could nod gracefully like the others.'

It found no pleasure in the sunshine or the birds or the red clouds that, morning, and evening, sailed overhead.

It was now winter and the snow lay round about white and sparkling, and when a hare came bounding along, it would often jump right over the little tree — and oh, how annoying that was! But two winters went by, and when the third came, the tree was so big that the hare had to go round it.

Oh, to grow, to grow, to be big and old! —
That, the tree thought, was the only pleasure in the world.

In the autumn the woodcutters came
and felled some of the biggest trees. This
happened every year, and the young fir-tree,
well grown by now, shuddered as the magnificent great trees fell creaking and
crashing to the ground. When the branches
were hewn off, they looked quite naked as
they lay there, long and slender and almost
unrecognizable. Then they were laid on
wagons, and horses dragged them away out
of the forest.

Where were they going? What was in
store for them?

In the spring when the swallows and
storks returned, the tree asked them, 'Don't
you know where they were taken to?
Haven't you come across them?'

The swallows knew nothing, but the
stork looked thoughtful, nodded his head
and said, 'Yes, I think so. I met many new
ships as I was flying from Egypt and they all
had fine new masts — I dare say they were
what you mean. They smelt of fir, and no
matter how many times I greeted them,
they kept their heads high, very high.'

'Oh, if only I were big enough to fly away
over the sea, too! — What actually is the
sea? What does it look like?'

'That would take far too long to explain,'
said the stork, and off he went.

'Be happy in your youth!' said the sun-
beams. 'Be happy in your fresh growth, in
the young life that's in you!'

And the wind kissed the tree and the
dew wept tears over it, but the fir-tree did
not understand them.

As Christmas drew near, quite young
trees were felled, trees that were often no
bigger and no older than the fir-tree of our
story which knew neither peace nor quiet
and was always wanting to be off. All these
young trees — and they were always the
most beautiful — kept their branches. They
were laid on wagons, and horses dragged
them away out of the forest.

'Where are they going?' asked the fir-
tree. 'They're no bigger than I am — in fact,
one was much smaller. Why do they keep
all their branches? Where are they being
taken to?'

'We know! We know!' twittered the
sparrows. 'We've peeped through the windows down in the town. We know where

they're taken. You can't imagine the brilliance and splendour in store for them! We've peeped in at the windows and seen them planted in the middle of warm rooms and decorated with the loveliest things — gilded apples, gingerbread, toys and hundreds of lighted candles.'

'And then?' asked the fir-tree, all its branches quivering. 'And then? What happens then?'

'Well, we haven't seen any more. But it was quite wonderful!'

'I wonder if I was born to travel such a brilliant road,' cried the fir-tree excitedly. 'It's even better than sailing over the sea. I'm quite sick with longing. If only it were Christmas! I'm tall now and well formed, with my branches stretching out like the others that were carried away last year. — Oh, if only I were on that wagon! If only I were in that warm room in all that splendour and glory! And then? — Yes, then something even better will follow, something even more beautiful — if not, why should they decorate me like that? Something even greater, even nobler, must come. — But what? Oh, how I suffer! How I long to find out! I don't know myself what's the matter with me.'

'Be happy with me!' said the air and the sunlight. 'Be happy in your fresh youth out in the open!'

But the fir-tree wasn't a bit happy. It grew and grew: winter and summer it stood there, green, dark green it stood. Those that saw it said, 'That's a lovely tree!' and towards Christmas it was the first to be felled. The axe struck deep through its heart, and the tree fell with a sigh to the ground. It felt pain and a sudden weakness. It was quite unable to think of happiness, it was so overcome with sorrow at being parted from its home, the spot where it had sprung up. It knew that it would never again see its dear old companions, or the little bushes and flowers around it, or even, perhaps, the birds. Its journey was by no means pleasant.

The tree was in the courtyard, unloaded with the other trees, before it came to itself and heard a man say, 'That's a fine one! That's the one for us!'

Two men-servants in full livery came and carried the fir-tree into a fine big room. Portraits hung round the walls, and by the great tiled stove stood large Chinese vases with lions on their lids. There were rocking-chairs, silk-covered sofas, great tables full of picture-books and covered with toys worth hundreds and hundreds of pounds — at least, that's what the children said. And the fir-tree was set up in a big tub filled with sand, but no one could see it was a tub because it was draped all round with green cloth and stood on a large brightly-coloured carpet. Oh, how the tree trembled! Whatever would happen now? Men-servants and young ladies came and decorated it: they hung little baskets cut out of coloured paper on the branches, and every basket was filled with sweets. Gilded apples and walnuts were hung up and looked as if they were growing there; and over a hundred little candles, red, blue and white, were fastened firmly to the branches. Dolls that looked really life-like — the tree had never seen anything like them before — swayed among the green needles, and right at the very top of the tree a big gold-tinsel star was fixed. It was magnificent, perfectly magnificent.

'This evening,' they all said, 'this evening it will be a blaze of light!'

'Oh,' thought the tree, 'if only it were evening! If only the candles were lit! And what will happen then, I wonder? I wonder if the trees will come from the forest to look at me? Will the sparrows fly up to the window? Shall I take root here and stand decorated, summer and winter?'

Yes, it could think of nothing else. It had a real barkache from so much longing, and a barkache is just as bad for a tree as a headache is for us.

Now the candles were lit. What radiance! What magnificence! The tree was so excited by it that all its branches quivered and one of the candles set fire to the greenery: the tree sweated with fright.

'Heaven preserve us!' screamed the young ladies as they hastily put it out.

And now the tree dared not give even the smallest quiver. What a dreadful moment it had been! It was so frightened of losing any of its finery and it was quite bewildered by all the brilliance — then the double doors opened wide and a crowd of children burst in as if they would overturn the whole tree. The grown-ups followed soberly. The little ones stood silenced — but only for a moment. Then they shouted for joy till the whole room rang with their noise. They danced round the tree as one present after another was pulled off.

'What is it they're doing?' thought the tree. 'What's going to happen?' The candles burnt right down to the branches, and as they burnt down they were put out. Then the children were given leave to strip the tree. My, they rushed upon it with such violence that all its branches creaked! If it had not been firmly fastened to the ceiling by its tip and the gold star on it, it would have been pushed right over.

The children were dancing around with their lovely toys, and no one looked at the tree except the old nurse who came peeping in among the branches, but that was only to see if a fig or an apple were still left.

'A story! A story!' shouted the children, dragging a stout little man over towards the tree. He sat down right under it. 'Now we're in the greenwood,' he said. 'And oddly enough, it may do the tree good to listen, too. But I'm going to tell only one story. Do you want to hear about Puss in Boots or about Humpty-Dumpty who fell down the stairs but for all that came to the throne and won the princess?'

'Puss in Boots!' screamed some; 'Humpty-Dumpty!' screamed others. There was such a shouting and a screeching, and only the fir-tree remained silent. 'Aren't I going to join in?' it thought. 'Aren't I going to do anything?' But of course it had joined in. It had done all it had to do.

And the man told them about Humpty-Dumpty who fell down the stairs but for all that came to the throne and won the princess. The children clapped their hands and cried, 'Tell us another! Tell us another!' They wanted 'Puss in Boots' as well, but they only got 'Humpty-Dumpty'. The fir-tree stood quite still and thoughtful. The birds out in the forest had never told him anything like that. 'Humpty-Dumpty fell down the stairs and for all that won the princess. Yes, yes, that's how the world goes!' thought the fir-tree, who believed it was all true because it was such a nice man who had told the story. 'Yes, who knows? Perhaps I shall fall down the stairs, too, and win a princess!' And it looked forward to being dressed up again the next day with candles and toys and gold and fruit.

'I shan't tremble tomorrow,' it thought. 'I'll enjoy myself properly in all my glory.

Tomorrow I shall hear the story of Humpty-Dumpty again, and perhaps the one about Puss in Boots as well.' And the tree stood there quiet and thoughtful the whole night through.

In the morning the men-servants and the maids came in.

'Now they'll begin to deck me out in my finery again,' thought the tree, but they dragged it out of the room, up the stairs and into the attic, and there they put it away in a dark corner where no daylight came. 'What's the meaning of this?' thought the tree. 'What am I supposed to do up here? What shall I have to listen to in this place?' And it leant up against the wall, and there it stood and thought and thought — and as the days and nights went by it had plenty of time for thinking. No one came up there, and when at last someone did come, it was only to put some big boxes away in the corner; the tree was now completely hidden and, one would imagine, quite forgotten.

'It's winter outside now,' thought the tree. 'The ground is hard and covered with snow. They can't plant me just yet, and so, no doubt, I'm to stay here under cover until the spring. That is thoughtful. Aren't people kind! — If only it weren't so dark here and so dreadfully lonely! — Not even a little hare! — Yes, it was very pleasant out there in the forest when the snow lay on the ground and the hare scampered by — even when he jumped right over me, though I didn't like it at the time. It really is dreadfully lonely up here.'

At that very moment a little mouse said, 'Squeak, squeak!' and nipped into the room. Then another little mouse followed and together they sniffed round the tree and scurried about among its branches.

'It's horribly cold!' said the little mice. 'But apart from that, it's a lovely place to be in. Isn't it, old fir-tree?'

'I'm not in the least old,' said the fir-tree. 'There are many who are much older than I am.'

'Where do you come from?' asked the mice. 'And what things do you know?' They were very inquisitive. 'Tell us about the loveliest place on earth. Have you been there? Have you been in the pantry where cheeses stand on the shelves and hams hang from the ceiling, where you can dance on tallow-candles, and go in thin and come out fat?'

'I don't know that place,' said the tree. 'But I know the forest where the sun shines and the birds sing.' And so it told them all about when it was young. The little mice had never heard anything like it before — they listened very attentively and said, 'My, what a lot you've seen! You have been lucky!'

'I?' said the fir-tree, and thought over what it had told them. 'Yes, I suppose they really were quite pleasant times.' Then it told them about Christmas Eve when it was decorated with cakes and candles.

'Oh,' said the little mice, 'how lucky you've been, old fir-tree!'

'I'm not old at all!' said the tree. 'It was only this winter I came from the forest. I'm at my very best — I'm just beginning to grow properly.'

'You do tell lovely stories!' said the little mice, and the night after they came with four other little mice to hear what the tree had to tell them, and the more it told them the more clearly it remembered it all and thought, 'Yes, they really were pleasant times. But they may come back, they may come back! Humpty-Dumpty fell down the stairs and yet won the princess. Perhaps I may win a princess, too.' And as it spoke, the fir-tree thought about a pretty little birch-tree that grew out in the forest and, in the eyes of the fir-tree, was a really lovely princess.

'Who's Humpty-Dumpty?' asked the little mice. Then the fir-tree told them the whole story — it could remember every single word. The little mice were ready to jump to the top of the tree with pure delight. The night after that many more mice came, and on Sunday two rats as well. But they said the story wasn't amusing, and that distressed the little mice because now they thought less of it, too.

'Is that the only story you know?' asked the rats.

'The only one,' answered the tree. 'I heard it on the happiest evening of my life, though at the time I didn't know how happy I was.'

'It's an exceedingly dull story. Don't you know one about bacon and tallow-candles? No pantry-tales?'

'No,' said the tree.

'Well, thank you very much,' answered the rats, and in they went.

At last the little mice stayed away, too, and then the tree sighed, 'It was really very cosy when they sat all round me, those nimble little mice, and listened to what I told them. Now that's gone, too. — But I shall remember to enjoy myself when I'm taken out again.'

But when would that be? — It happened one morning when they came rummaging in the attic. The boxes were moved and the tree was pulled out. They threw it down on the floor — pretty hard, too — and then one of the men dragged it away towards the stairs where the daylight shone.

'Now life's going to begin again,' thought the tree. It felt the fresh air and the first rays of the sun — and then it was out in the yard. Everything happened so quickly that the tree completely forgot to look at itself, there was so much to see all round. The yard adjoined a garden where everything was in bloom: roses hung fresh and sweet-scented over the low fence, lime-trees were in flower, and swallows flew about saying, 'Tweet-tweet-tweet, my husband's come!' But they gave no thought to the fir-tree.

'Now I'm going to live!' it cried joyfully,

stretching out its branches — but alas! they were all withered and yellow, and it lay in a corner among the weeds and nettles. The gold paper star, still in place at the tip of the tree, glittered in the bright sunshine.

Two or three of the merry children who had danced round the tree at Christmas and been so delighted with it, were playing in the yard. One of the smallest of them came and tore the gold star off.

'Look what's still left on the ugly old Christmas-tree,' he said, as he trampled on the branches snapping them under his boots.

The tree looked at the flowers, beautiful and fresh in the garden — it looked at itself, and wished it had stayed in its dark corner in the attic. It thought of its own fresh youth in the forest, of the merry Christmas Eve and of the little mice who had listened with such delight to the story of Humpty-Dumpty.

'Gone! Gone!' said the poor tree. 'If only I'd been happy when I could! Gone! Gone!'

And the man-servant came and chopped the tree into small pieces until a whole pile lay there. It blazed beautifully under the big copper; and it sighed so deeply, each sigh like a pistol-shot, that the children who were playing ran in and, sitting down in front of the fire, looked into it and cried, 'Pop! Pop!' But with each crack — really a deep sigh — the tree thought upon a summer's day in the forest or a winter's night when the stars were shining. It thought of Christmas Eve and Humpty-Dumpty, the only fairy-tale it had ever heard and knew how to tell — and then the tree was burnt up.

The boys played in the yard, and the smallest of them wore upon his chest the gold star which the tree had worn on its happiest evening. It was gone now, the tree was gone, too, and its story was over — over and done with, as all stories are, sooner or later.

The girl shepherd

'But, sir, that's not fair!' I said.

I've been going along to drama club all term to get noticed and then he goes and shunts me off to be a shepherd.

Deirdre was picked to be virgin. Some virgin! Deirdre's so daft I don't think she even knows what the word means. She's pretty enough, but she has this peculiar way of talking and I know that's why sir chose her. To build up her confidence. Deirdre has this vacant look on her face most of the time too.

But when she heard she'd been chosen, for a moment she seemed quite lit up. I don't really mind about Deirdre. I didn't want to be the virgin Mary anyway. But I did want to get something decent.

'Why can't I be one of the kings?' I said. The kings get to wear all the best clothes and they don't have to learn long speeches. They just come trailing in while the choir sings.

'Because girls can't be kings', said sir, and everybody tittered. 'And another thing, scripturally speaking, they weren't kings. They were learned men.'

Sir chose Brian Lo for a king. Now he really is a wise man of the East. He's our brainbox from Hong Kong.

Roman soldier, I wouldn't have minded that, or Herod's dancing girl with a yashmak and a naked navel. Or an angel.

Anyone without a key role was shoved off to be a boring old shepherd abiding in the fields, or else a townsperson.

'Blimey!' I said. 'There's going to be more shepherds than sheep on that hillside.'

'All right, Tracey, then you can be a townsperson.'

'No thanks, sir. You said shepherd. I'll stick with shepherd. But whoever heard of a female shepherd?'

'You'll manage.'

I felt annoyed all the way home, but consoled myself with a chocolate creme Father Christmas from the corner shop.

Shepherd stupid. I bet I'll have to carry a furry lamb and wear a teatowel tied round my head.

After that, I always took a book with me to rehearsals and made to look as though I was deeply absorbed in reading it. As far as I could see, there was no point in me being there anyway, since the shepherds didn't have anything to do except hang around and listen to the angel Gabriel getting the giggles every time Deirdre had to say that the baby leaped in her womb. But sir said we all had to attend because it helped the main characters get used to the atmosphere if everybody was there from the start. Some atmosphere!

Finally, sir got really annoyed with me for not joining in.

'Why pick on me?' I said. 'There's others been messing about more than me.'

Two of the kings had been playing the fool all the time.

'Tracey, it's your negative attitude. It's affecting the others.'

'All right then,' I said. 'I won't be in your stupid play. Nativity's for infants anyway.' And I got up to stomp out of the hall.

'Oh no you don't, my girl,' he called and dragged me right back in. 'It's too late for that. If you hadn't wanted to be chosen, you should have said so at the start. You can't do a bunk now.'

So we had a bit of a row, me screaming at him about my rights which I felt a bit bad about because of poor Deirdre. There she was in the middle of her flight into Egypt, gaping with her mouth open, not understanding what was going on. She's got a starring role and she doesn't even realize that her husband's had this dream and been warned to leave the country.

After I'd called sir a jumped-up berk he sent me to the deputy head's office.

Actually, I'm not frightened of her. She

looks like a dry old bird but at least she always knows you by name when she's dishing out punishments.

She offered me a peppermint lump across the desk and asked what it was all about. I explained to her. 'And see, I'm just fed up with it, that's all. I'm in drama and everything. I could've been great if he'd given me a chance. If he'd let me choose a proper part. I know I could. A credit to the school.'

She listened. She's good at listening. Then she said, 'And if you could choose your own part, what would it be?'

I thought a bit and realized there aren't enough roles for girls. Unless sir had decided to have all Herod's wives. He had nine. Every time he got fed up with one, he sent her off to the harem and took a new one. He never even tried to make a go of it. Playing one of those nine wives, discarded in the harem, would have ended up a bit like playing a shepherd, just one of the herd.

'I dunno, miss,' I said. 'I just wish I'd been able to choose something a bit more, well, you know.'

'Significant? Of course you do. But I wonder, Tracey, if we any of us are ever able to *choose* our parts? If we're lucky, we are chosen but it's seldom the role we'd have picked for ourselves. D'you think Mary wanted to have a baby in a stable, even if it was going to be you-know-who? And Herod didn't choose to be king. He *was* king. His choice was limited to what he did with that position.'

'Yes, miss.'

'And what counts most is what we do with the roles we're cast in.' She gave me another peppermint lump. 'Now I believe, Tracey, that if you set your mind to it, you can make something of this shepherd. So off you go, back to the others.'

Well blow me! A goody lecture wasn't what I was expecting. Dinner duties till the end of term I'd thought. Christmas charity must have affected her brain.

So I went, chewing my mint, and meek as a lamb, to join the rest of them at Mrs Philps' room to get kitted out. All shepherds and all townspeople were told to go and stand out in the corridor while the chief roles, virgin Deirdre, Joseph, Balthazar, Melchior, Caspar, Herod, Elizabeth, and Gabriel went in. Their costumes were more complicated. And I knew exactly what it would've felt like to be one of Herod's wives, discarded, out in the place of disfavour.

Then Graham as well, who's playing Joseph, was sent out to stand with the rest of us riff-raff.

'Not you yet, dear,' Mrs Philps said. 'Joseph is costumed like the shepherds.' What, no halo even? Poor old Joseph. He looked quite mystified.

The first two kings came out, cockahoop with their crowns and caskets, treasures and robes, followed by Brian Lo full of Eastern promise.

'And who have we here, dear?' said Mrs Philps when my turn came at last. 'Angel?'

'Shepherd,' I said, 'And if you don't mind, I'd rather not have to wear a teatowel on my head. I really want to be a girl shepherd.' I thought it was worth trying on.

Mrs Philps seemed quite pleased with that. 'What a nice accommodating lass you are. Because if you'd wanted to be just the same as the others I'd have had to run up something new. As it is —.' She took a shapeless striped garment off a hanger and pulled me into it, then took a huge dark veil from a drawer. 'Bit the worse for wear and not a very flattering colour, I fear.' It was brownish grey.

'Actually, that's all right,' I said, because I was going to *look* as though I was trying if that's what deputy head wanted. 'I mean, if I was a real shepherd from a shepherd's family, I wouldn't be dressed in good stuff, would I?'

Mrs Philps had a knack with the veil, wrapping and tucking neatly and quickly so that when she'd done I looked like one of those Arab women you see shopping in London. I felt great. Sort of invisible in there, yet myself. So when the rest of the kids went on at me, I didn't mind too much.

'Oooer, Pharoah's mummy, is it? Or little brown riding hood?'

I didn't mind the teasing but I felt it was my duty to explain one or two facts to them which had just occurred to me.

'Listen, you guys,' I said. 'It doesn't actually *say* in the Bible that it was only men shepherds. It could just as easily have been women too. Women do heavy jobs in China and Russia, so why not in the Holy Land? And another thing —.' When only your eyes are showing and the rest of your face is smothered in veil people seem to listen better. 'I bet when the shepherds first saw that angel, I bet you, it was a girl shepherd who said. "Hey, folks let's go and take a peek." The angel never told them to go. They just went of their own accord. And you want to know why? Because, basically, women are more interested in babies being born than men are. Left to their own devices, the fellas would have just gone on lying there in the dark listening to their sheep munching.'

Some of them laughed but I told myself I wouldn't mind. People often laughed. They laughed at Graham for being husband to Deirdre when she was already pregnant. But Joseph hadn't chosen who to marry. Deputy Head was right there. The angel had just told him what he'd got to do.

Up till the real show, we practised in the school hall. But on the Big Night, we were to go to the parish church in town because it's more central for parents. Mum gave me early tea, then she said, 'Here, Tracey, you'd better take these,' and gave me some satsumas out of the fruitbowl, and untied a couple of chocolate Santas off our tree.

'What for? I've had my tea.'

'Oh, you never know. But after all, it is nearly Christmas.' Mum knows I'm a sucker for chocolate cremes.

My sister said, 'Like me to do your face for you?'

But I said, 'No thanks' and explained about being just an ordinary shepherd who wouldn't have worn make-up. Of course, if I'd been the dancing girl with rubies in my navel and diamonds in my nose that would've been different. But I'm not. So there we are.

Outside, it was a very ordinary sort of night for an ordinary shepherd — cold and foggy, with steaming, overcrowded buses full of late-night shoppers. When I got to the parish church I half regretted the make-up. You should've seen some of the angels! Hair-gel spikes, frosted lips, blushers, rainbow eye-tints, all bright against their white robes. They looked terrific.

Sir said, 'Well, they say there's room in heaven for all sorts.'

We shepherds weren't going to be on for ages, because first there was all the bit with Deirdre having to struggle with the Annunciation, and her long journey to Bethlehem. So once we were costumed, Mrs Philps showed us to a side chapel where we were all to wait. We could hear the shuffling of people arriving, and the winter coughing, and the expectant whispering. We could feel things going on out there but we couldn't see. It's very frustrating to know something important is happening and not be there.

The vicar had put this little bar fire to keep our feet warm but it was still freezing. And boring.

'Didn't know it'd take this long,' said Terence. He was number one shepherd. I was about number seventeen.

Being cold and bored at the same time makes people dead hungry. I thought about my girl shepherd. She'd have known it'd be flipping cold on that hillside and she'd have known how we'd all get flipping hungry.

I went and felt in my coat pocket.

'Hungry, shepherds?' I said, very casual.

'Oh yerer,' said Terence. 'Whadyergot?'

I'd have liked it to be barley bread, olives, and dried figs, wrapped in vine leaves. But satsumas and chocolate pretties off the tree did all right. Good old shepherd's Mum.

You should've seen those shepherds' faces! Were they pleased! I shared out the food fairly, and then tidied up because you can't go leaving litter around in side chapels, any more than you can on Judean hillsides.

And, at last, sir, with shaded torch, was beckoning us to follow him to be ready for the angel Lesley to tell us the good news. I thought, my golly, it isn't half dark. The lighting was so dim you could hardly see where you were going. Almost spooky. You think of Christmas as being a time of bright lights and sparkle, and here was this church in gloom. Bit mean, I thought, even if the country is going through hard times, to save on proper lighting. And with all these people here too.

The place was completely full, not just parents, but others too, and lots of them having to stand at the sides. So we had to push our way through the crowd to be able to harken to the herald angel and begin our way along the main aisle.

A little voice in the choir was singing, thin and high like a shooting star. *Puer natus a boy was born in Bethlehem.* Then the singing choirs of angels joined in with glorious exultations and all the church lights began to come on, not in a sudden flash so you'd get a migraine, but gradually like a sunrise, till brightness filled the air and you could see the clear colours of people's woolly hats, the redness of holly berries, the rich yellow of chrysanthemums, the shine of the angels' faces. It wasn't anyone being mean with electricity. It was part of the arrangement.

'Come on, Tracey,' whispered shepherd number one. 'Keep up.'

Alleluia! Alleluia! Puer natus!

When we were at the middle of the church and the angel Lesley pointed us towards a stable, I was surprised to find I believed in it all. I felt as though we really were on a windy hillside going to see something new.

The deputy head had said to me, 'Tracey, to be part of this play, you've got to pretend you're touched by grace, even if you aren't.'

'Yes, miss,' I'd said, though I hadn't a clue what she'd meant.

I still didn't really know. But whatever it was, I felt that this was probably it. And I knew it was real and important because one of the smaller shepherds, Larry from first year, got the feeling too.

'Hey, Trace,' he said, pulling at my veil.

'Great, isn't it? Really feels like something's happening and we're in it?'

I nodded, and he grinned, and we hurried on towards the manger side by side.

After the show was over, everybody surged for mince-pies and coffee. People and performers, staff and pupils, juniors and uppers, enemies and friends. And kids who normally won't even *look* at each other, were chatting away and smiling and eating. We were all there, and we were all together. And I thought, it doesn't matter if one girl shepherd understands what happened tonight, or not. All that matters is that I am here and I am part of it.

Baldur

Baldur dreamed. Dreams invaded his sleep so that he woke trembling and cold. The gods were not used to nightmares and Baldur should have been the last to suffer them. Baldur was the wisest and best-looking of the gods. He was so gentle and kind that nothing evil could live near him. He seemed to shine out, even among the gods.

Loki was, of course, jealous of Baldur. Loki was the second handsomest in Asgard. Loki was clever rather than wise. Loki was not gentle or kind. Evil seemed to grow up near him. His jokes and tricks went wrong and even his friends had grown cold towards him.

If Loki had had bad dreams no one would have been surprised, least of all Loki himself. Perhaps he did, and kept quiet about them. Baldur was surprised and tried to describe his dreams to the other gods. All he succeeded in doing was to worry them with forebodings of disaster. He painted images of flickering red, like fire, like serpents. He described feelings of piercing, like roots growing into his body. Above all he filled their minds with the suffocating blackness that smothered him in his sleep. Fear swallowed them up. No one knew what they were afraid of, but they were all afraid for Baldur. The most afraid was Frigg, Odin's wife, for she was Baldur's mother. She questioned him and questioned him about his dreams but all he could talk about was flickering red, piercing, blackness.

When Frigg talked to Odin, the All-Father was vague and said nothing to calm her. He talked of Fate and of the Well of Urd.

The great Ash Tree, Yggdrasill, had its roots in three springs, one each for the worlds of the gods, the giants, and the dead, Asgard, Utgard and Hel. By the spring in Asgard, which was called the Well of Urd, sat the three maidens who wove the fate of the worlds, the Norns.

Frigg could not sit and do nothing. She left Asgard and went through the worlds. She made everything she met swear an oath that it would not harm Baldur. Everything she asked swore that it would do Baldur no harm, and swore readily because he was loved by all — all except Loki.

Frigg went first to anything that might have been in Baldur's dreams: the red flickering flames of fire, the shimmering coils of serpents. She went to everything that could pierce: to the trees whose wood makes spears, to the iron which the dwarfs beat into swords, to stone which anyone can make jagged and throw. She then went to likely and unlikely things: to grass on which he might slip, to water which could drown him, to fog in which he could lose his way and wander until exhausted. All swore that they would not harm their golden god.

Frigg returned to Asgard. At dinner that night she told Baldur that he had nothing to fear.

'Everything in all the worlds has sworn not to hurt you. Dream no more, my son.'

'Let's try then,' said Loki and threw his drinking-horn straight at Baldur's head. The horn fell to the ground before it could touch him. Loki, smiling outwardly though raging inside, grabbed everything within reach and hurled it with all his strength straight at Baldur. It all fell to the ground without touching him: plates, jugs, knives, stools, all fell harmlessly. A feeling of excitement and release from tension swept through the gods and they all hurled things at Baldur while he sat smiling happily. This became an evening's entertainment for the gods when they had drunk enough, but nothing ever touched Baldur enough to hurt him. Loki was hurt, though, as Baldur became the gods' chief entertainment.

Baldur did not tell his mother that his dreams continued for he believed that she had done everything that she could. Frigg did not ask for she was reassured every

evening by the game of Aunt Sally that the gods played.

But Loki noticed Baldur's haggard face in the morning — and noticed how he smiled when his mother was near.

One evening after dinner in the Hall of Asgard an old woman hobbled in and sat down next to Frigg. She started talking of her children and of all she had done for them. Then she watched the gods throwing at Baldur and the conversation seemed to turn inevitably to Frigg's journeys to make him safe.

'And did you really visit every single animal, and plant, and . . . and . . . thing?' the old woman asked. 'My goodness, that was a task indeed. How long did it take you?'

Frigg described her journeys through the worlds and talked of the oaths she had received from everything.

'And did you ask every last thing in the worlds?' probed the old woman.

'Well, no,' said Frigg, lowering her voice and glancing round to see if Loki was near. 'There was a small bush growing west of Valhalla called mistletoe that was . . . well, I thought it was too small and young, and just too far away to be any threat to Baldur.' Frigg did not say that she feared the ancient magic of the mistletoe that grew green and flourishing amid the winter deadness of the great oak tree.

'Did you really visit Valhalla?' interrupted the old woman, rather hastily, as if she wanted to change the subject. 'Surely no woman is allowed there? What is it like?'

'You must remember that Odin, my husband, is Lord of Valhalla. That is why I was able to go there on my quest. It has a wonderful great Hall roofed with shields and there go all those who die in battle. The Hall has more than six hundred and forty doors for I lost count there. Each door is wide enough for nine hundred and sixty men to march out of to battle.'

'Who can they fight in that dead land?' asked the old woman.

'They fight each other all day until they are all killed. In the evening they all come to life again and go back to the Hall for feasting, drinking, and long stories of their greatest battles. Odin told me,' Frigg said, leaning forward and speaking confidentially, 'that he is keeping these warriors in training for the last great battle.'

'But what can they find to feast on in that dead land?'

Frigg did not like the way the old woman kept talking of the dead land but she answered, 'They eat roasted boar which, like Thor's goats, come back to life again each morning. Their drink is the most intoxicating mead. It flows from the udder of a goat that stands all day on its hind legs and tears at the buds on the great tree that grows there. So much mead flows from her that there is more than enough for all the warriors.'

'It sounds better than the dread land of Hel,' said the old woman, 'and that is where those who do not die in battle will go.'

As Frigg had spoken of Valhalla she had forgotten her indiscretion in the pleasure of remembering the sights she had seen. The old woman said farewell and hobbled out of the Hall again and Frigg smiled fondly at the gods amusing themselves throwing at Baldur.

Loki was not seen in the Hall of Asgard for several days. The first god to know of his return did not see him at all, for it was blind Hod who heard him first. Blind Hod stood smiling while around him the other gods threw at Baldur.

'Why don't you throw something?' whispered Loki in Hod's ear.

'I have nothing to throw,' Hod replied. 'And, besides, how would I know where to throw?'

'I will help you,' whispered Loki. 'Here, hold this twig.'

Loki placed his branch of mistletoe in Hod's eager hand and turned him until the blind god could aim straight at Baldur.

'Now!' he whispered.

At that moment Baldur looked up and saw through the crowd the light flickering red on Loki's hair. A terrible suspicion flashed into his mind. But Hod had thrown

the mistletoe, sharpened by Loki, and it went clean into Baldur's body. Baldur felt it pierce his chest like roots growing into an oak tree and then ... blackness overwhelmed him and he dropped like a felled oak, dead.

Making the most of it

For twelve days and nights
The Christmas Tree that I bought last year
Stood unwatered and undernourished
In a flower-pot in the drawing-room.
How could we know what it felt,
Hung with coloured globes and tinsel,
Gifts and candles;
Pulled and poked about and fingered
By eager children;
Wreathed with smoke from cigars and cigarettes
And fumes of wine and punch?

When the Feast was over
I took a chance.
And carefully replanted the tree in my garden,
Tenderly spreading the parched and aching roots,
Not daring to think he might live
But he did.

Now he comes back into the house again,
Like an old servant called in for a special occasion,
Glad to be made use of,
Beaming upon the company from the serving table.

Of course I am not sure I have done the right thing.
He may catch cold, or catch warm (which is worse),
For it can't be good for trees to be dug up annually
And draped with 'frost', and tinsel,
Gleaming balls and candles,
And made to stand in sand for twelve days and nights.

We shouldn't like it if we were Christmas trees!
The only thing to do is to give him a third chance
And hope he will take it.

William Kean Seymour